Dear Reader,

I hope you will enjoy this book "A Runaway Star" in hardback.

So many of my friends have asked if they could have it in hardback as they want to keep it and often refer to it as an almost ideal love story.

I think you will find it is something you will return to and enjoy especially when you are tired and need the inspiration of love and beauty which I try to give to you always in my books.

It comes to you with my love,

BARBARA CARTLAND

A RUNAWAY STAR

SEVERN SH HOUSE

JLJC SR

This first hardcover edition published in Great Britain 1987 by
SEVERN HOUSE PUBLISHERS LTD of
4 Brook Street, London W1Y 1AA

British Library Cataloguing in Publication Data
Cartland, Barbara
A runaway star.
I. Title
823'.912 [F]   PR6005.A765
ISBN 0–7278–1297–1

Printed and bound in Great Britain
at the University Printing House, Oxford

Author's Note

Queen Victoria had her life threatened six times during her reign. On May 29th, in her own words she noted: "a little swarthy, ill-looking rascal pointing a pistol, which at two paces misfired." The rascal slipped away into the crowd. The Queen felt certain he would try again and could not bear to have the danger 'hanging over her'.

Telling none of the household, the Royal couple drove out the next day exactly as before but the Queen thoughtfully left her Lady-in-Waiting, Lady Portman, behind. "I must expose the lives of my gentlemen," she said, "but I will not those of my ladies."

The man fired again at five paces. He was condemned to death but reprieved on July 1st, because the pistol was not loaded. Another attempt was made two days later by a deformed boy only four feet tall. Fortunately his pistol was loaded generously with paper and tobacco and very little gunpowder.

In February 1872 the sixth attempt was made by a weak-minded youth with the idea of frightening the Queen into releasing some Fenian prisoners.

John Brown, the Queen's Scottish ghillie, seized the man, and was afterwards rewarded by Her Majesty with public thanks, a gold medal and £25 annually. "I was trembling very much and a sort of shiver ran through me," the shaken Queen reported.

Chapter One
1842

Millet put on his green-baize apron and sat himself down at the Pantry table on which he had already arranged a number of pieces of silver.

This was the time of night which he really enjoyed when he had sent the footmen to bed and could be on his own.

Millet was an expert cleaner of silver using the ball of his thumb the way he had been taught when he was a footman.

He had improved on and elaborated his technique all through his life until any silver that passed through his hands had such a brilliant sheen that it reflected everything else on the Dining-room table.

Tonight Millet was giving himself a special treat and had taken from the huge safe, that was the size of a small room, a silver cup with a rock crystal bowl that had made him draw in his breath in admiration the first time he saw it.

Designed by Sir Martin Bowes in 1554 it had not seen the light of day, he was sure, for many years.

It had certainly needed cleaning despite the fact it was wrapped in green baize and Millet had passed his hand over it in the manner that a man might touch the body of a woman he loved.

Silver, in fact, was Millet's real love and it had almost broken his heart when he had to leave the Earl of Sheringham's collection which he had cleaned and prized for nearly thirty years.

He did not want to think about that now, but to concentrate all his admiration on the treasures he was continually unearthing in his new place.

He knew in his heart they would soon obsess him and he would think of them both by day and by night.

The silver cup with its ornate chasing on the top and round the base, with figures of naked goddesses upholding the stem and the Goddess of Mercy surmounting the whole, was the finest example of its kind that Millet had ever seen.

He felt as if his thumb itched to start work and he mixed the white cleaner in a saucer stirring it until it was as fine as milk.

Then he picked up the clean piece of linen he had ready to use.

At that moment there was a knock on the Pantry door and Millet raised his head impatiently.

He was a distinguished-looking man and the younger members of the household had often teased him saying he looked like a Bishop.

Now, with a distinctly un-Christian note in his voice, he asked:

"Who is it?"

As if the question was an invitation to enter, the door opened and the night-watchman, a man as old as Millet himself, put his head round the door.

"Oh! It's you!" Millet said ungraciously. "Well, I'm busy. No time for a chat this evening!"

"There's a visitor to see ye, Mr. Millet."

"A visitor?" Millet questioned, the irritation still in his voice.

The one thing he really disliked was being interrupted when he was concentrating on his silver-cleaning.

Before he could ask who on earth would be likely to visit him at this hour, a slight figure pushed past the night-watchman and came into the Pantry.

Millet looked up in astonishment, for it was a woman with a veil over her face and he could not imagine who she could possibly be or why she had come to see him.

Then, as the night-watchman closed the door, the visitor threw back her veil. Millet gave an exclamation and rose to his feet.

"M'Lady!"

"You are surprised to see me, Mitty?" a young voice answered. "I know it is late, but I felt sure you would not have gone to bed."

"No, M'Lady. But you oughtn't to be out at this time o' night."

Millet pulled out a chair from the corner of the room as he spoke, dusted it with the corner of his green-baize apron and set it down near his visitor.

"Sit down, M'Lady," he invited.

The girl – she was really little more – did as he requested.

But she first unfastened the dark riding-cape which she was wearing over a velvet habit and then pulled off the high-crowned riding-hat.

She laid it down on the table beside the silver cups, and tidied her hair with her hands.

It seemed as if the sunshine had come into the darkness of the Pantry. The light from the oil lamp picked out the strands of gold in her fair hair and seemed to linger in her large expressive eyes.

They were strange eyes, blue, but the pale blue of a thrush's egg.

Her eyelashes curled back from them like a small child's, darkening at the tip to give her the expression of someone very young and Spring-like.

Looking at her one felt instinctively that human problems and difficulties of the world had never touched her and never should.

"You've not come alone, M'Lady?" Millet asked.

Having disposed of her outdoor garments, she turned her face to his with a smile on her lips.

"I rode here on Caesar. He is outside tied up to a post."

"Alone! On Caesar, M'Lady! You know His Lordship wouldn't like that!"

"His Lordship will not like a number of things I am doing, so one more will not matter!"

There was a note in Her Ladyship's voice that Millet had not heard before and he looked at her apprehensively.

He thought as he did so that His Lordship would be wise to worry a little more about a daughter who was as beautiful as Lady Gracila.

But Millet had learnt in the hard school of domestic service that the employer was always right, and he waited in silence.

He knew Lady Gracila would explain to him why she had come to visit him at an hour when she should have retired to bed in her room on the second floor at Sheringham Castle.

"Sit down, Mitty," Lady Gracila said, using the nickname she had given him when she was a child.

It brought back so many happy memories that old Millet felt like crying for the old days which could never return.

"Sit down, Your Ladyship?" he asked in surprise.

"Oh! Mitty, stop being so respectful and standoffish. I want your help, as I wanted it when Mama died and you were the only person who could comfort me."

There was a little throb in Lady Gracila's voice which was very moving.

Millet sat down as she requested, looking at her anxiously. He thought she appeared a little pale and not as happy as he would have wished.

"What's troubling Your Ladyship?" he questioned in a sympathetic manner which had never failed to coax her problems out of her, even when she was no higher than his knee.

Lady Gracila drew in her breath.

"I have run away, Mitty." ·

"But Your Ladyship can't do that!" Millet exclaimed, "your wedding's in a few days' time!"

"I cannot marry the Duke! I cannot!" Lady Gracila declared. "That is why you have to help me, Mitty."

She saw the old Butler was stunned and after a moment she went on :

"I waited until the house was quiet. Then I left a note for Papa on my pillow and crept down the back stairs. Caesar came when I whistled, I bridled and saddled him and rode off to find you!"

"But, M'Lady ..." Millet began, only to be interrupted as Lady Gracila continued :

"I do not intend to go back, so I was not so foolish as to come empty-handed. I brought some of my best gowns with me on Caesar's back and a holland bag with everything else in it I thought I would need, hanging from the pommel."

Millet stared at her almost open-mouthed.

"But, M'Lady, you can't stay here."

"I have to, Mitty. You do not understand, this is the one place where they would never think of looking for me."

She gave a little laugh which had no humour in it.

"It would never strike Papa for a moment that I would do anything so reprehensible as to come to Barons' Hall!"

"But, M'Lady ..." Millet began.

"I know you are going to argue, Mitty," Lady Gracila said, "but before you do so please fetch my gowns and other things from Caesar's back. They are everything I now possess in the world and I do not want him shaking them off or trying to roll."

Millet opened his mouth to protest, but Lady Gracila circumvented him by saying in a pleading tone which was irresistible :

"Please, Mitty. Please, dear Mitty, do what I ask."

With a sigh he went from the Pantry closing the door behind him.

When he had gone Lady Gracila put her hands up to her face as if it was a gesture of defence.

"I have to stay ... here," she told herself. "Where else could I ... possibly go where they would not ... find me? Besides, I have ... very little money."

She had thought desperately before she left the Castle where she could obtain some.

But there had never been any reason for her to have more than a sovereign or so in her possession at a time and a few silver shillings to be used for the collection in Church.

She had, however, brought what pieces of her mother's jewellery were not in the Pantry safe.

It was impossible for her to lay her hands on the rest, for the new Butler was not like dear old Mitty, and would doubtless have refused to let her take them out of his care without first having permission from her father.

She had tried to be practical, tried to think of everything before she actually left her home.

But all the time, forcing her, compelling her, hurrying her away was the conviction that she must escape and never ... never ... could she marry the Duke.

Now, looking back she saw how gullible and foolish she had been to allow herself to be persuaded into accepting him in the first place.

That had been her Step-mother's doing and Gracila acknowledged that she had been clever in getting her own way with so little opposition.

She was an astute and intelligent woman and Gracila realised now that in comparison she herself was nothing but an ignorant and credulous child.

It had seemed so exciting to be sought out by the Duke of Radstock and informed that she was to be his wife.

It was a position that Gracila knew to all the girls of her acquaintance would be the height of their ambition.

The Duke was not only one of the most important Noblemen in the country and the richest, he was also a sportsman and his race-horses had carried his colours first past the winning post in nearly every classical race.

"The Radstock diamonds are fantastic, better than the Queen's," her Step-mother had said.

She had spoken beguilingly, but there had been a note of envy in her voice which she could not prevent.

"You will be an hereditary Lady of the Bedchamber," she went on. "You will attend every State Ball, and it is said that the Queen has a very soft spot in her heart for the Duke! But then it is well known that Her Majesty loves handsome men!"

It was all very alluring.

Gracila loved horses, and having always lived in a large Castle she was not overawed by tales of the Duke's huge Mansions filled with treasures collected down the centuries.

She was a little disappointed that as a suitor he had approached her father before first ascertaining what were her feelings about becoming his wife.

But then, she told herself in good common sense, it would never enter his mind that anyone should refuse him; for he was undoubtedly the greatest matrimonial catch in the whole of the British Isles.

Her Step-mother had glossed very briefly over the fact that the Duke had been married before.

After all, his wife was dead and what was the point of dwelling on the past or on the fact that he was old enough to be her father.

Because Gracila's imagination had carried her away into dreaming of life as a Duchess, she had not really thought about the Duke as a man and a husband.

Instead he had seemed a rather nebulous being, like one of the mythical heroes of the past.

They had always been more real to her than the people she met in everyday life.

Being so much younger than her brothers and sisters, and therefore so much alone, Gracila found her companions in the books that she read with such avidity.

Her Nurses and Governesses were continually warning her that she would wear out her eyes.

"Read! Read! Read!" her Nanny had said often enough, "you'll be blind as a bat by the time you're my age, you mark my words!"

Gracila had not listened. She knew that books stimulated her imagination and carried her away into Fairyland where everything was beautiful and happy.

And there were certainly no disagreeable women with sharp voices like her Step-mother to hurt her.

It was not only that the new Countess of Sheringham was taking her mother's place in the house; it was not that she was jealous of losing her father's attention; it was that instinctively Gracila was aware that Daisy Sheringham was not a nice woman.

She could not explain even to herself what her instinct told her. She only knew that however hard she had tried to overcome it she shrank from any contact with her Step-mother.

She should therefore have been suspicious from the very first when she told her she was to marry the Duke of Radstock.

'I was blind ... completely blind ... like a kitten which had not ... opened its eyes,' Gracila thought now.

But that, she told herself, had made the shock of realisation all the worse, and she still felt almost physically sick as she had when the truth had been revealed to her only this afternoon.

The Duke had come to stay at the Castle to make the final preparations for their wedding.

Gracila had seen very little of him up to date. In fact, as was customary where very young girls were concerned, she had never been allowed to be alone with him except for the few minutes when her father had sent for her to come to the Red Salon and she had found he was there with the Duke.

Gracila had not even known that the man whom she

had been told was to marry her was in the Castle.

She had therefore not only been surprised to see him, but felt shy as she walked down the room conscious that he was watching her.

She had curtsied politely but still felt too embarrassed to raise her eyes to his.

"Your Step-mother will have told you, Gracila," her father had said, "that the Duke of Radstock has done you the very great honour in asking for your hand in marriage. He wishes to speak to you and I am therefore going to leave you alone."

The Earl walked from the room as he spoke and Gracila, with her heart beating in a manner which was disturbing, stood waiting still with her eyes lowered.

"I am sure we will be happy together, Gracila," the Duke said, "and I hope you will like the ring I have brought you."

He had taken her left hand in his as he spoke and put on her finger an enormous diamond ring which seemed almost too heavy for it.

"Thank ... you. It . it ... is very ... lovely," she managed to say although it was difficult to speak.

"It has been in my family nearly five hundred years," the Duke said, "and there is a necklace and tiara to go with it which you will be able to wear after we are married."

"That will ... be very ... nice."

The Duke did not speak and because she was surprised by his silence Gracila raised her eyes to his.

He was looking at her in a manner she found strange because it was almost as if he was inspecting her – looking for something, although she had no idea what it could be.

Then he said with a smile :

"You are very beautiful, Gracila. I feel sure you will be acclaimed as one of the most beautiful Duchesses of Radstock, and there have been many of them."

"Th . thank . . . you," Gracila said simply.

There was a little more warmth in her voice than there had been before and she suddenly wondered if he would kiss her.

Instead he raised her hand to his lips and as he did so her father came back into the room.

She tried later to discover for herself what she thought about him.

He was certainly good-looking but his complexion was that of an elderly man, his hair grey at the temples, and his figure had not the athletic slimness of a young man.

"Would I have liked him to kiss me?" Gracila asked herself.

It was strange, she thought, that she really had no feelings in the matter.

She had never been kissed, but she had imagined as an expression of love it would be very wonderful.

But how? And what sort of feeling would a kiss evoke?

In the books she had read of every sort and type, and especially those that were written in France, love was deeply emotional.

It also seemed to be a rapture which drove those who felt it to do valiant deeds, to achieve the impossible and even to sacrifice their lives.

"Could I feel like that for the Duke?" Gracila asked.

And when he left the Castle the next morning she still did not know the answer.

Today, when he had returned a week before the wedding, she was determined to get to know him better.

All through the fittings for her trousseau which filled almost every hour of the day Gracila was occupied only with her secret thoughts.

She found it hard to concentrate on the presents which arrived at the Castle in great profusion; the hundreds of letters of congratulations, and the endless chatter from her Step-mother about her future life.

Marriage had always seemed a goal to which she had been propelled ever since she was old enough to leave the Nursery and move into the School-room.

"You must concentrate on arithmetic," her Governess would say sharply, "otherwise what will happen when your husband finds you cannot keep the household accounts accurately?"

"You wait until you're married and have children of your own, and then you'll understand," Nanny would say when she queried some Nursery rule.

They really seemed to talk of nothing else: Nanny who had stayed on when her Governess came; the Governess who had obviously been told to prepare her for her adult life; and her Step-mother who was continually finding fault with her appearance.

"I shall never get you a husband, Gracila, if you walk about looking like a gypsy!"

"Men hate clever women and no husband wants one! So stop reading and go upstairs and find some sewing to do!"

Everything anyone said seemed concerned with the man who would eventually marry her.

Gracila thought that when he did come he would be a perfect gentle Knight, like Sir Galahad, adventurous like Ulysses and as compellingly attractive as Lord Byron.

Secretly, because her Governess had not approved of Lord Byron's poems, she read them in the Library as she did a number of other books which would have been taken out of her hands had she been discovered with them elsewhere.

"Is the Duke like any of these men?" she wondered.

Because she felt she must have some standard to measure him by she slipped down to the Library to take *A Collection of Lord Byron's Verse* from the shelf.

She knew only too well that if anyone found her reading it at this time of the day she would be told to do something else.

There was a place in the Library she had made especially her own.

At the far end of the great room which had been designed by Robert Adam there was a long window ornamented in coloured glass with the bearings of the Sheringham family.

It was framed with red velvet curtains which did not pull back closely against the wall and therefore provided between them and the window a perfect hiding-place from anyone who entered the room casually.

The wide window-seat was also covered in red velvet and Gracila had curled up in the corner with a cushion behind her back to open the leather-bound book with a feeling of delight.

It was 'Don Juan' that she studied first.

"Love rules the camp, the Court, the grove – for love
Is Heaven, and Heaven is love."

'Could the Duke make her feel like that,' she wondered.

Then, because the answer frightened her, she turned over the pages quickly, wanting to look at her favourite verse from 'The Vision of Judgment'.

"The angels all were singing out of tune,
And hoarse with having little else to do,
Excepting to wind up the Sun and Moon,
Or curb a runaway young Star or two."

Smiling because the picture the poem always painted amused her, she was brought back to reality by the sound of two people talking at the far end of the Library.

Concentrating on the poems, she had not heard them enter, and now she recognised her Step-mother's voice and answering it was a man's she knew to be the Duke.

'They are not likely to discover me,' Gracila thought complacently.

She went on reading, not wishing to listen to anything they were saying.

It was only when she heard her own name mentioned that she raised her head.

"Gracila is so young, so unsophisticated, that she would never be suspicious unless someone told her," her Step-mother remarked.

Gracila wondered what she would be suspicious about.

"No-one is likely to do that," the Duke said. "Youth and innocence are a protection in themselves."

"I am sure you are right and it will be wonderful to be able to see you without any difficulties. We can stay with you and you can come here."

The Countess gave a deep sigh and added:

"Oh! darling, these years have been hell without you!"

Gracila was suddenly tense!

Could she have really heard her Step-mother say such words and speak in a voice she had never heard her use before?

"We must be very careful," the Duke said.

"Of course!" the Countess cried, "but tonight, my darling, we will be safe, I promise you."

"Here? With George in the house?"

"He has a cold and he is sleeping in his own room. I will come to you, and, oh, Andrew, if you only knew how much I want and need you!"

"My poor Daisy, but we could not go on as we were and how could I have guessed that Elsie would die only six months after you were married?"

"The fates were against us," the Countess said with a little sob in her voice, "but now I shall see you again! If you only knew how I have missed you. There has never been a man as handsome and as attractive as you."

She paused a moment, then she lowered her voice to say passionately:

"No-one! No-one in the world could be a more marvellous lover!"

Gracila felt that she was turned into stone.

Then there was silence and she knew the Duke was

kissing her Step-mother. A moment or so later she heard the Library door close and knew that she was alone.

She sat very still and her mind felt numb, unable to grasp what had happened, unable to understand what she had heard.

Then she faced the truth.

The Duke was her Step-mother's lover and had been so before she had married her father.

When her father had married again it had never struck Gracila that her Step-mother was desirable not only as a wife but as a woman.

She had read, mostly in the books that were in French, of middle-aged women who sought love dramatically and generally tragically, but somehow she had never envisaged that applying in her own home.

Her father was a somewhat stern man and because she was the baby of the family he had always seemed very old even when she was a child.

Her mother had loved him and had always been happy but when he married for the second time the Earl had treated his wife, who was so much younger than himself, rather as if she was a child he had to protect and spoil.

Gracila's mother had never been very strong after her birth but she still looked surprisingly young and at times very like her youngest daughter.

Only when she had died did Gracila realise what a perfect companion her mother had been and how lost and lonely she felt without her.

It was then the Earl had been captivated by a very determined and sophisticated woman.

Daisy supplied in his life, even in his old age, everything he had missed without knowing it, in the sweet, gentle childishness of Elizabeth.

But now Gracila realised why instinctively she had mistrusted her Step-mother and why so often the things she said had rung false.

When finally she rose from her hiding-place in the Library she felt as if her limbs were suddenly stiff and she had grown immeasurably older since she had taken down Lord Byron's poems from the shelf.

She replaced the book exactly as she had found it.

Then as she looked at where she thought her Step-mother and the Duke had stood as they kissed each other, she knew that never, never would she consent to marry a man who did not love her.

"How could they behave in such a manner?" she asked herself and shivered because she was suffering from the shock of what had happened.

She had gone up to her bedroom and because she did not wish anyone to know what she was feeling when the time came to change for dinner she did so in the usual manner.

She had gone downstairs feeling as she watched her Step-mother and the Duke that she was seeing a very unpleasant plot unfold itself on the stage and she alone was in the audience.

Her father was being charming, playing host with a geniality which told Gracila how glad he was to have anyone so important as the Duke for his son-in-law.

'If only he knew!' she thought to herself.

For the first time she looked at her Step-mother not as someone in authority over her but as an immoral woman, and saw her attractions even though she hated her for displaying them!

Now she was aware, watching for it, that there was something in the way the Countess spoke, the expression in her eyes, and the manner in which she moved her white shoulders which was very revealing.

But it was significant, Gracila admitted, only to someone who had the key to the puzzle, the plan of the maze.

When she was upstairs wondering what she could do to save herself from a marriage which was too horrible to contemplate, she knew the only possible solution was to run away.

How could she hurt her father by telling him the truth, and how would anyone listen to her unless she did so?

She was well aware that any protests she might make that she did not wish to be married would be put down to nerves and maidenly modesty.

Her objections, unless she could substantiate them, would be pushed aside.

She would find herself being taken up the aisle to marry a man who had no interest in her as a person except that she would make it easy for him to make love with her Step-mother!

Gracila felt that knowing what they intended to do tonight she could not bear to be in the Castle.

She felt, although she slept a floor above her Step-mother in a different part of the building, she would still be listening for a woman creeping along the darkened passages to the room of the man who was her lover.

"I must run away! I must disappear," Gracila decided.

The difficulty was, where could she go.

None of her relatives would shelter her, they would be appalled that she could jilt anyone so important as the Duke, and at the last moment.

Her friends came into the same category and she thought how angry the ten bridesmaids that had been chosen by her Step-mother from all the most important families in the country would be!

Gracila shivered.

They had all bought and paid for their expensive dresses; the flowers for their bouquets had been ordered; the brooches which were to be their bridesmaids' presents consisting of the Duke's initials and hers entwined under a coronet had already arrived at the Castle.

The tenants, after the ceremony, were to be entertained in the great tythe barn and the huge barrels of ale were already in place, as were the trestle tables at which they would sit for a wedding-feast.

How could all that be cancelled?

She only knew it had to be!

There was only one way by which to make sure the marriage did not take place and that was to vanish.

If there was no bride, the whole machinery that would have been put into operation for the marriage ceremony would have to come to a halt.

All through dinner the same question was asking itself over and over again in Gracila's mind.

"Where can I go? Where can I go?"

Some other part of her brain watched the smiling curve of her Step-mother's lips; saw a glimpse of something unpleasant in the Duke's eyes, heard her father droning on about the political situation.

"Champagne, M'Lady?"

The note of impatience in the Butler's voice made Gracila realise that he had already offered to serve her.

Then suddenly she remembered – Millet!

It was her Step-mother who had sent away old Millet because she did not like him and alleged he did not do his work properly.

Millet had always been part of the family and it was inconceivable that after nearly thirty years at the Castle he should be dismissed.

But her Step-mother preferred servants who would give their loyalty to her rather than to the Earl.

Now Gracila thought that perhaps there was another reason.

Servants always knew too much; servants talked! Those she engaged herself would not be shocked by anything she did and would certainly never betray her.

The thought of Millet was like a life-line to a man drowning in a dangerous sea. Next to her father and mother Gracila had loved Millet more than anyone else in the world.

One of the first words she had spoken was 'Mitty', holding out her arms to him as she was trying to walk.

Whenever she could escape from her Nanny she would be found in the Pantry sitting on Mitty's knee and looking at the silver he got out of the safe especially to show her.

He spoilt her with grapes from the big bunches fresh from the Greenhouses. The gardeners would never send in fruit for the Nursery.

"Mitty will hide me," Gracila told herself.

She felt as if the thought of him swept away the darkness which had enveloped her like a frightening cloud ever since she had known she must leave the Castle.

She knew where Mitty had gone when he had said good-bye with tears streaming down his face.

In his ordinary clothes, he had looked a shabby old man instead of the awe-inspiring Bishop-like Butler he had always seemed when he welcomed guests in the Hall or was on duty in the Dining-room.

"What will you do? Where will you go, dear Mitty?" Gracila had asked.

She found it hard to believe that anyone who was so familiar and so much a part of her life could be so easily expendable.

"I'll find another post, M'Lady," Millet had answered. "For the moment I'm going to stay with my sister."

"Mrs. Hansell at Barons' Hall?"

Millet nodded because the lump in his throat made it hard for him to speak.

"But when you leave there you promise you will let me know your new address?"

"I promise, M'Lady."

"And you will take care of yourself."

"I shall be thinking about you, M'Lady. I'll always be thinking about you."

"And I will be thinking about you, dearest Mitty," Gracila had answered.

As she had spoken she had flung her arms round the old man's neck and kissed him as she had done when she was a little girl.

She did not care what anyone thought or said. Mitty was part of her life. Mitty belonged as her Step-mother never would.

Her action had made him speechless.

He had slipped away to where, outside the kitchen door, a gig was waiting to carry him and his piteously small amount of luggage away from the only home he had known for over thirty years.

"How could you let Step-mama sack Millet! Millet of all people, Papa?" Gracila had asked her father when she had first heard what was happening.

"You know I never interfere in household affairs, Gracila," her father had replied coldly.

"But Millet has been here all my life and he came as a footman before you married Mama!"

"Your Step-mother says that he is past his work," the Earl replied.

"That is not true!" Gracila stormed. "Everyone praises the silver the moment they come into the Dining-room, and you know as well as I do that anyone in the County would rather have a footman from here trained by Millet, than from anywhere else!"

"I am not prepared to discuss it, Gracila. I leave all those things in your Step-mother's hands."

It was a weak answer and Gracila knew her father was feeling uncomfortable. Without another word she had gone out of the room and slammed the door.

It was very unlike her as Gracila seldom lost her temper, finding when her mother was alive, no cause to do so.

In her own room she had cried and cried as she had not done since her mother's funeral because she knew when Millet had gone she would be even lonelier than she had been before.

"Why could I not have thought of him at once?" she

asked herself and felt that now everything was simpler.

Somehow, though it was impossible to think how, Millet would solve her problem as he had, all through her life, solved so many others.

* * *

The Pantry door opened and Millet came back.

He carried over one arm a big bundle made by Gracila's dresses tied up in a silk bed-cover which she had thought was the best way to convey them.

They had in fact been no trouble to keep in place lying over the front of her saddle.

In his other hand was a big holland bag in which the housemaids at the Castle put the hand-towels when they were dirty.

They were left in the Housemaid's cupboard until they were collected by the odd-man who took them down to the washerwomen who worked in the Castle Laundry.

It was quite heavy, but Caesar was a strong spirited horse which Gracila had trained since he was a foal, and he could have carried ten times the weight without it making any difference to his pace or stamina.

Millet laid the gowns along the seats of two chairs which stood behind the Pantry door and put the holland bag down on the floor beside them.

He then moved towards Gracila and she knew, when she saw the expression on his face, he was going to be difficult.

"I've brought these in, M'Lady," he said in his gentle voice, "because you asked me to do so. But as soon as you've rested, I'm putting them back on your saddle and sending you home."

"I have no intention of going, Mitty," Gracila said, "and there are ... reasons ... reasons I cannot ... tell you, but I swear to you there are very real ones why I cannot marry the Duke."

Millet looked at her sharply.

He had known her all her life and now saw what he

had not noticed before, an expression in her face that told him she had suffered some shock.

He wondered what could have happened?

Whatever it had been, he was aware that the little girl he loved more than anyone else in the world, although she was hiding it, was deeply upset.

"It's her Step-mother!" he told himself perceptively and said aloud : "If you wants to get away, M'Lady, you can go to your grandmother. She's always loved you."

"And what advice do you think she would give me, Mitty, except to marry the Duke!"

Gracila took a deep breath. Then she put out her hands towards him and drew him to her so that he sat down once again beside her.

"Listen, Mitty," she said, holding on to him, "you know I trust you and you must trust me. I swear to you that there is nowhere and no-one except you who would not at this moment force me to return to the Castle and marry the Duke."

Millet's eyes were on Gracila as she went on :

"But I know you will believe me when I tell you I would rather die. It would be wrong and wicked for me to marry the Duke, and I know that if Mama was alive she would tell you the same."

Gracila waited and then she asked :

"Do you believe me, Mitty?"

"I believe Your Ladyship, but what's the alternative?"

"I want you to hide me! Hide me here at Barons' Hall where no-one will think of looking for me until the row over my disappearance has died down and the Duke has accepted the situation."

"But I can't do that, Your Ladyship!"

"Why not?" Gracila asked, still holding on to his hands.

"Because His Lordship's come home. He's in residence!"

"Lord Damien!"

"Yes, M'Lady, he arrived three days ago!"

Chapter Two

For a moment Gracila was astonished into silence and then she said:

"I can hardly believe it! He has not been home for twelve years!"

"That's true, M'Lady."

"And he has really returned?"

"Yes, M'Lady. He's come from Italy."

Gracila nodded, it was what she might have expected.

Over the past few years there had always been people who had mentioned that they had seen Lord Damien in Paris or Vienna, but most often in Rome, Venice, Palermo, Naples and a dozen other places in Italy, that she herself had always longed to visit.

Whenever people spoke of him it was always with a strange note in their voice.

Gracila had long ago identified this with the knowledge that they were shocked, but at the same time found it thrilling to talk about him.

She had been too young to understand what had happened when the scandal first broke in the County.

She had been only six at the time, but looking back it had seemed to her that all through her life Lord Damien had been a subject of conversation, not only between the adults in the Drawing-room but in the Servants' Hall and the Nursery.

She had often thought that people talked in front of children as if they were deaf or half-witted.

It had therefore not been long before she connected something mysterious, secretive and at the same time ex-

citing with the young man who was the heir to Barons'
Hall.

At first she was only aware he had done something terrible and horrifyingly wicked. She imagined he had committed a murder or stolen some priceless treasure.

Then gradually she began to understand that the wickedness involved a woman.

Snatches of conversation were revealing.

"He had always been wild, of course, but I never thought anything like that would happen!"

"Can you imagine anything so utterly disgraceful? She was in attendance on Queen Adelaide only the month before!"

Then later Gracila heard:

"My dear, I saw them in Paris at the Opera, as bold as brass, and she was wearing the most fabulous jewels!"

"Of course, there is no doubt that he is madly attractive and just like Lord Byron, but – to run away!"

It was therefore fixed in Gracila's mind that the young man who had lived only five miles away at Barons' Hall looked like Lord Byron.

Although at first she was unconscious of doing so, she began to collect scraps of what she heard and fit them together almost like a puzzle.

Finally she learnt the whole truth!

Not from her mother who never talked scandal, but surprisingly from her father when his old friend, Lord Damien, died.

"Damn it! I feel ashamed that his only son was not present at his funeral!" he said, throwing his crepe-trimmed high hat down on the table. "I believed that that young reprobate would have come home whatever had happened in the past!"

"I heard," Gracila's mother replied in her soft voice, "that Virgil was in India."

"Well, all I can say is he should be at home doing his

duty! It is intolerable that one of our nearest neighbours should be a man with his reputation!"

When Gracila was alone with her father later that evening, she had asked him a little nervously:

"What has the ... new ... Lord Damien ... done, Papa, which makes you and everyone else speak of him so harshly?"

"He has offended the proprieties beyond redemption!" the Earl replied.

"In what way, Papa?"

Her father hesitated, as if he thought she was too young to be told. Then he answered:

"You may as well know the truth, for if you do not learn it from me, you will find it out from someone else!"

"People are always talking about ... him, Papa."

"That is not surprising!"

"What did he do that is so very wicked?"

Again her father hesitated before he said harshly:

"He ran away with the Marchioness of Lynmouth!"

Gracila had stared at him wide-eyed.

She knew how important the Marquess was and she had sometimes visited with her parents his huge ancient Mansion which had always seemed to her awe-inspiring, but cold and unwelcoming.

"You ... mean the present ... Marquess's ... wife?" she asked after a moment.

"She was younger than he and a foreigner," her father said abruptly. "One can never trust these foreign women, but that does not excuse Damien for behaving like a cad!"

Gracila had been able to extract no more information from her father, but now she was in the possession of the key to the puzzle she could weld the other pieces together.

The late Lord Damien had one son, Virgil, who had been spoilt abominably, so her Nanny had always said, by his mother. He was talented and brilliant in many other ways, but wild and far too handsome "for any woman's peace of mind".

It was inevitable that women would fall in love with him as had the Marchioness of Lynmouth.

Apparently everyone had known when they met clandestinely, riding together in the woods where they thought no one would see them, and walking through the shrubberies hand in hand.

Of course there had been the prying eyes of gamekeepers, gardeners, women from the Village and a host of others to discuss what they had seen.

The only two people who were quite unaware of what was occurring were the Marquess and Lord Damien.

For them it had been a shock like the explosion of a bomb-shell, when it was learnt that the Marchioness and young Virgil had run away together.

The whole County was agog, with tongues wagging, noses almost touching as they gossiped and chattered.

They chewed over and over every scrap of information they could find and then waited breathlessly, as if watching the curtain rising on a play, to see what the Marquess would do.

He did nothing!

He did not shut himself away, but continued with his usual work in the County, attending meetings and committees.

He patronised, as he always had, sports meetings and entertainments and civic or social functions which had customarily taken place in his house.

He neither discussed nor mentioned what had taken place with anybody.

His behaviour was proud, distinguished, honourable and applauded by Gracila's father.

"I would not have given Lynmouth credit for having so much self-respect," he had said to his wife in Gracila's hearing.

She could understand how disappointed people were

31

who had expected him to behave dramatically.

"You would have thought," her Governess said to Nanny, "that a gentleman like the Marquess would have fought a duel for the return of his wife."

"Perhaps he doesn't want her back," Nanny replied.

"He can never marry again unless he divorces her," the Governess had said almost wistfully.

"If you ask me," Nanny answered, "His Lordship has had enough of women to last him a life-time, and you can't blame him with a wife like that!"

Gracila noticed that while the ladies like her mother and her friends blamed the Marchioness, the gentlemen all took up the attitude that young Virgil had made a fool of himself.

"The hot-headed young idiot!" she heard a hunting Squire say forcefully, when he did not know she was in the room. "What the devil did he want to run for when he could have enjoyed the spoils of the chase without leaving home?"

It did seem strange, Gracila thought when she grew older, that the heir to Barons' Hall and his father's title should still be living in exile. For she had learnt that the Marchioness with whom he had eloped so sensationally, with the passing of time, had left him and they were no longer together.

It was a year after his father died, a year she would always remember in which her father married again, that there began to circulate a fresh batch of rumours about the new Lord Damien.

"He is a huge success in Paris," one of her Step-mother's friends related. "I saw him when I was there at one of the smart parties I attended. The next night he was at the Theatre with a woman who had every man in the audience staring at her rather than at the stage!"

"Who was she?" Gracila's Step-mother asked.

Her friend shrugged her shoulders.

"One of the *grandes cocottes* with whom Paris abounds.

My dear, you have never seen anything like their jewels! They left one breathless!"

The conversation turned to clothes and jewellery, but anyone who had travelled on the Continent always seemed to have seen Lord Damien.

When she heard he was in Italy, Gracila envied him.

How she longed to be in the sunshine and to see the magnificent statues and buildings she had read about in her books, the Borghese Gardens, the Trevi Fountain, the Colosseum, St. Peter's!

In her imagination they were a background for a man who looked like Lord Byron and who was talked about in very much the same manner.

Had not her favourite poet had to flee the country because he was involved in so many scandals!

Lord Damien's was the same story, and now, incredibly, when everyone had given up ever expecting him to return home, he was there!

She realised that while so much had flashed through her mind, Millet was waiting.

"Your Ladyship sees the position," he said when she had not spoken, "and if you'll take my advice, M'Lady, you'll go home and tell His Lordship you've no wish to marry His Grace. I feel sure you can make him understand."

"His Lordship would not understand, and I cannot possibly tell him the reason why nothing ... nothing in the ... world, would make me marry the Duke!"

Gracila spoke passionately and as she did so she saw a new understanding in Millet's eyes.

'He knows!' she thought. 'He must have known before he left that Step-mama is not what she pretends to be!'

Millet might not have known about the Duke, but he had accompanied her father and Step-mother when they went to London for the Season every year.

They used to open the rather gloomy house in Hanover Square for two months while Gracila had been left in the country.

If there was one lover in her Step-mother's life, there might easily have been more and the servants would have known about it because servants always did.

Millet did not speak and Gracila knew she had silenced him from trying to persuade her to return home.

"You do see, Mitty," she said after a moment, "this is one place no one will look for me, especially if His Lordship is here. After all that has been said in the past, I doubt if he will be overwhelmed with callers."

"That's what I thinks, M'Lady," Millet agreed. "At the same time how could you stay in a house alone with a gentleman, and especially His Lordship? It'd ruin you, M'Lady!"

"If people knew about it, I quite agree," Gracila replied, "but no-one will know and nor will His Lordship!"

"You mean, Your Ladyship, that you expects me to hide you?"

"Why not?" Gracila asked. "Barons' Hall is big enough to hide a regiment if necessary! What is more, from all I have heard about him, it is doubtful if His Lordship will stay long."

It would be far too dull, she thought, for a man, who from all reports was more at home at parties or even orgies, whatever they might be, than in the country.

"I have heard of the fantastic orgies he gives at his palazzo in Venice," her Step-mother had said with what, Gracila thought, was a note of envy in her voice.

"Orgies?" the friend to whom she was speaking questioned. "Orgies? What happens at his orgies?"

"That is what I long to know!" the new Countess had replied. "Emily will be returning next week and we must find out from her. Emily always knows everything!"

But her Step-mother had visited Emily instead of vice versa and Gracila had never heard the end of the story.

Now she said aloud in a positive tone.

"I am certain, Mitty, that His Lordship will not stay long and then you can relax and just keep me hidden away from Papa."

"I can't do it, M'Lady!" Millet said in anguished tones. "It's not that I don't like deceiving Your Ladyship's father, who's always treated me like a gentleman. It's also that I've no wish to lose my new job."

"I heard that you had become the Butler after old Temple died."

"Yes, M'Lady, Mr. Baines, the Agent, asked me to take over his duties which weren't arduous as there was no-one in the house."

He paused a moment before he said:

"I'm getting on in years, M'Lady, and it'd be difficult for me to get another position."

Gracila gave a little cry.

"Oh! Mitty, how could Step-mama have sent you away? It was cruel, and I cried and cried when you left!"

"She had her reasons, M'Lady."

"I am sure she did!" Gracila replied in a hard voice.

Again Millet gave her a sharp glance before he said quietly:

"If you can't go home, M'Lady, we must think of somewhere else."

"There is nowhere," Gracila replied. "I have thought and thought. There is nowhere I can go, especially as I have no money."

"No money!"

"I have some of Mama's jewels, the ones I was wearing. But even if you sold them for me, I would be ... afraid to be ... alone in London."

"It's unthinkable, M'Lady! Absolutely unthinkable!"

Gracila smiled.

"Then I am afraid, Mitty, you will just have to put up with me."

The old Butler looked at her and knew there was nothing else he could do. How could he let this beautiful child – Gracila in his eyes was nothing more – go alone into a world of which she knew nothing?

The idea of what might happen to her made him shiver.

He decided that if hiding her meant he had to starve, then that would be a small price to pay for the happiness she had brought him ever since she had been a baby.

"Mit...ty! Mit...ty!"

He could see her struggling towards him looking like a small, fat cherub, her pale blue eyes shining, her small cupid-bow lips smiling.

Then some years later crying on his shoulder.

"I hate...Nanny! I told her the...truth but she won't ...believe me!"

There were so many more pictures of Gracila stored in Millet's mind: a child coming to him with problems about her Governess; a girl crying helplessly and desperately because her mother was dead.

It seemed to Millet, looking back, that his whole life had centred round his silver and Lady Gracila.

He loved them both so devotedly it was difficult to think of them except linked with each other.

It was for Gracila as a baby that he had taken the small pieces out of the safe and let her smudge them with her little fingers. It was for the little girl that he had described the wonders of the pieces made by Hans of Antwerp, goldsmith to Henry VIII.

As she grew older he had showed Gracila how to recognise the craftsmanship of Paul de Lamerie, Platel and Paul Stour.

All great artists in silver, but it struck him now that Lady Gracila was pure gold and a treasure beyond price.

"I'll hide you, M'Lady," Millet said suddenly making up his mind. "But Your Ladyship must swear to me that you'll keep out of sight of His Lordship."

"You know I will do that, Mitty dear, for I would not wish you to get into trouble," Gracila said. "Thank you ...thank you from the bottom of my heart! I knew you would not fail me."

"I don't approve, M'Lady, of what I'm doing, mind you," Mitty said earnestly, "as Her Ladyship knows, a good servant's loyal to him who pays them, and His Lordship'll expect me to be as straightforward to him as I'd expect him to be with me."

"I hardly think His Lordship is in a position to criticise what happens in his house considering he has neglected it for so long," Gracila replied.

Then a thought struck her.

"Has His Lordship come alone?"

"He's brought only his Valet with him, M'Lady, a man who's been with him ever since he grew up. I knows him, Dorkins comes from the next Village."

Gracila thought it was interesting that the man who had stayed with the wicked reprobate all these years came from his own County and had lived at home!

She had just been about to say so when she realised that Millet had a certain expression on his face. She remembered that when he was organising a party or ordering his footmen about, he assumed an air of authority which made him quite awe-inspiring.

Then he was not a bit like the gentle, kind, understanding Mitty to whom she always turned in trouble.

She waited and Millet said:

"If you'll wait here, M'Lady, I'll go and fetch my sister. She'll have to be let into our secret, but no-one else."

"But of course," Gracila cried. "I can trust Mrs. Hansell as I trust you."

Millet left the Pantry and Gracila sat down, looking for the first time at the treasures spread out on the table.

It was what she might have expected, she thought, to find Mitty cleaning his silver late at night when everyone else had gone to bed.

Because she had finally got her own way and Millet had agreed to hide her, she suddenly felt weak and exhausted.

The shock of what she had experienced this afternoon, combined with the urgency to get away from home, made her feel now as if she would like to cry.

It was all so horrid and sordid: her Step-mother having

a love affair behind her father's back, confident that the Duke's marriage to her would effectively disguise their liaison.

It might have deceived her father, but Gracila wondered how long they would have deceived her?

Then she told herself that unless she had over-heard what they had said in the Library it would never have occurred to her in a million years to be suspicious.

How could she imagine that the woman who had married her father and taken the place of her mother, would ever behave in such an immoral manner?

Or that the Duke, who was a gentleman, would marry with the object of continuing his affair with his mistress.

Gracila felt besmirched, somehow unclean.

Then she told herself she must try to be sensible and understand that people did behave in such a manner. It might seem incomprehensible, but it was a part of human frailty.

She had read about such situations in books but they had not seemed real. She had never envisaged it could happen to people like her father or herself.

'I suppose it is because really I am very young and ignorant,' she thought.

The Pantry door opened and Mrs. Hansell came in.

She was an elderly woman with a kind face, very like her brother's, and she was wearing, as Gracila had expected, a black dress and from her waist hung a silver chatelaine.

The keys attached to it tinkled as she walked quickly towards Gracila.

"M'Lady! M'Lady!" she exclaimed. "I can't believe that you're here!"

"I am not only here, Mrs. Hansell," Gracila answered, "but as Mitty will have told you, I need your help."

"He's told me, M'Lady, but I don't know what your Lady Mother would have said, that I don't!"

"If Mama were alive, I promise you, Mrs. Hansell, she

would understand why I have had to run away and why I know the only place I can be safe is with dear Mitty, and of course you."

"Well, M'Lady," Mrs. Hansell said, "I've known you since a baby and I couldn't be refusing your plea for help, or turning you from the door. But I'm only praying I'm adoing the right thing."

"I shall be safe with you and Mitty, Mrs. Hansell, and that is all that matters."

Gracila saw by the expression in Mrs. Hansell's eyes that she had struck the right note.

It was her safety that these dear people were worried about.

"Well, I'll put Your Ladyship in a room near me," Mrs. Hansell said briskly as if, having made up her mind, the sooner they got on with the arrangements, the better.

She looked towards the roll which contained Gracila's gowns lying on the two chairs behind the door and the holland bag standing beside it.

Then she exclaimed:

"I've a better idea! If I puts Your Ladyship in the Elizabethan room at the far end of the East Wing, and sleep next door, you'll be well away from the rest of th' household."

She paused before she went on.

"So far, as His Lordship has only just returned, I've only a few elderly women working with me whom I can trust as I trust m' own hand. But I may have to bring in others, an' women talk, as you well know, Your Ladyship!"

"Indeed, I do," Gracila smiled, "and I would love to be in the Elizabethan Room."

She knew the house well because when her father used to visit old Lord Damien in the last days of his life, she would often ride to Barons' Hall with him.

Then, while the two gentlemen talked, she would visit Mrs. Hansell and as often as not would be taken on a tour of the house.

There was plenty to see.

Barons' Hall had received its name from the Barons who had gathered there at the time of the Magna Carta, the Lord Damien of the day being descended from those who invaded England with William the Conqueror.

The house through the centuries had been burnt down and rebuilt and little remained of the original austere home of the early Barons.

But the result was now an amalgamation of centuries from the huge State Rooms added in the early Georgian times to the small low-ceilings and diamond-paned windows of the Elizabethan period.

It was this part of the house that Gracila thought enchanting and she doubted if the new Lord Damien, even if he entertained huge parties, would use the East Wing.

Visitors had always been more impressed with the big four-posters in the State Bedrooms, their ostrich fronds rising towards the painted ceilings.

They had admired the carved gold pelmets, many of which had been designed by Adam, surmounted by Georgian windows with their square panes.

As Gracila followed Mrs Hansell up the back stairs and then along the twisting corridors which grew narrower towards the Elizabethan Room, she felt as if she was stepping back into the past.

And she was in fact a fugitive as the Jesuit Priests had been from the fire and torture of Elizabeth, or the Royalists who had lain concealed in the house while Cromwell's soldiers searched it.

Finally they reached the room at the furthest end of the corridor and Mrs. Hansell tipped the candle with which she had led their way to light those on the dressing table.

"I've been thinking, M'Lady," she said as she did so. "What we could say to explain Your Ladyship's presence in th' house."

"Perhaps I could be your niece, Mrs. Hansell?" Gracila suggested.

"That's very flattering," Mrs. Hansell smiled, "but I can assure Your Ladyship, you don't resemble any of m' nieces who have called here over th' years to see me."

Gracila remembered they had also called on Millet, and they were large, strapping young women with countless children.

"What I thinks would sound more plausible, M'Lady," Mrs. Hansell went on, "would be that you should be a Lady of Quality, which indeed Your Ladyship is, fallen on hard times."

"If you mean penniless, Mrs. Hansell, that is exactly what I am!" Gracila said.

"Before I comes here nigh on fifteen years ago, Your Ladyship," Mrs. Hansell continued as if she had not spoken, "I was in service wi' Sir Ronald Deering. A nice gentleman he were too."

"I remember hearing Mitty say that that was whom you were with in London."

"Then Sir Ronald got into trouble, M'Lady," Mrs. Hansell went on, "gambling was one reason, bad investments of his money another! So th' house was closed, th' staff sent away and that was why I comes here."

Gracila was listening.

She guessed what Mrs. Hansell was going to say to her, but she knew the House-keeper did not like being hurried.

"Now suppose, M'Lady," Mrs. Hansell suggested, "I were t' say that you are one of Sir Ronald's grand-children, who, after his bankruptcy and death, has no-one to support her."

"I think it is a wonderful idea!" Gracila exclaimed, "and I have only to remember that my name is Deering, which is not very difficult. Clever Mrs. Hansell! I am so delighted you are able to think of such a good story!"

"I'm glad Your Ladyship approves."

"I am sure Mitty will be too," Gracila remarked. "I will also be able to explain tomorrow why Caesar is here. After all, Sir Ronald's impoverished grand-daughter might still possess a horse!"

41

"That's not to say, M'Lady," Mrs. Hansell said quickly, "that His Lordship must ever be aware of your presence. We can trust Thomas, whom Millet is awaking at this moment, to see to Caesar. He's a cousin o' ours by marriage."

"Then Thomas will be trustworthy," Gracila smiled.

"And I myself 'ill talk to Cable in the morning," Mrs. Hansell continued. "He's a good man though a bit slow in the uptake."

Cable was the Head Groom who had been at Barons' Hall ever since Gracila could remember.

After her tour of the house, if her father was not ready to go home, she had always gone to the Stables.

Cable had taken her round the stalls providing her with a basket of carrots with which to feed Lord Damien's horses.

"They are in splendid condition, Cable," she would say at the end.

"Oi thinks Your Ladyship'd be pleased wi' 'em," Cable would say slowly.

That was about the extent of his conversation and Gracila thought they could be quite certain of one thing, that Cable would not reveal her presence in the Hall!

Mrs. Hansell unwrapped the silk bed-cover from Gracila's gowns and hung them one by one in the wardrobe.

They looked exceedingly decorative and had cost what to Gracila seemed an astronomical amount, but her Stepmother had been determined that she should be dressed in a manner which befitted a Duchess.

'I doubt now,' she thought to herself, 'if anyone will see me in them, but at least I shall have the pleasure of wearing them!'

It suddenly struck her that if later she had to find some way of keeping herself and earning money, they would be a most unsuitable attire for a Governess or Companion.

There were no other careers open to a lady, and Gracila thought it unlikely she would ever be fortunate enough to obtain such a position.

42

As if Mrs. Hansell was aware of what she was thinking, she said as she began to unpack the holland bag:

"Now don't you worry about th' future, M'Lady. Perhaps things in a day or so'll seem better than they do at th' moment."

"I doubt it," Gracila answered in a low voice. "Papa and Step-mama will be expecting me to return before the wedding even though I have made it quite clear that I will not marry the Duke!"

"There'll certainly be a commotion, right enough!" Mrs. Hansell remarked.

Then, holding one of Gracila's pretty lace-trimmed night-gowns in her arms, she said:

"Is Your Ladyship quite certain you're adoing th' right thing?"

It was almost, Gracila thought, as if the elderly woman thought she had to make a last appeal for her to do what was expected of her.

But she knew perceptively that at the same time, Mrs. Hansell, like Millet, had some idea of why she had run away.

"I cannot ... marry the Duke, Mrs. Hansell," she said in a low voice, "and I have no intention of returning home until Papa and His Grace have accepted the... truth."

"Very well, M'Lady, if that's your decision, we'll not speak of it again," Mrs. Hansell said. "We must just hope that no-one's likely to come alooking for you here."

"It is the last place they will look," Gracila said positively.

"I hope Your Ladyship's right," Mrs. Hansell answered in a tone of voice which proclaimed she was quite certain she was.

When at last Mrs. Hansell had said good-night and Millet, who Gracila was sure still thought of her as a small child, had brought her up a glass of warm milk and some chocolate-covered biscuits, she was alone.

She undressed slowly, delighting, as she did so, in her

surroundings, as the light of the candles revealed the mellowed panelling on the walls, the hand-embroidered short velvet curtains which covered the small windows, and the carved oak head-board of her bed.

It was as if the room told her that all the troubles and difficulties she was experiencing at the moment would eventually matter as little as those of the Elizabethan members of the Damien family who had slept there.

"Perhaps they had been afraid!

"Perhaps they had run away!

"Perhaps they too had to fight for what they believed was right!" Gracila told herself and the idea was comforting.

As she got into bed she felt she was surrounded by gentle ghosts who would watch over her and keep her safe.

But as she shut her eyes she found herself thinking of Lord Damien in another part of the great house and wondered what he was feeling.

"Is he glad to be here?" she asked, "and why has he come back after all this time?"

They were questions which seemed for the moment to supersede her own problems.

How strange it must have been to live away from England and everything that was familiar for twelve years.

It meant, Gracila knew, that Lord Damien was now thirty-one years of age, for he had been nineteen when he had run away with the Marchioness.

She had been older than he, and despite the prejudiced description of her which Gracila had heard from her Nanny and the Governesses, they had all agreed that she was beautiful.

Again she had pieced together tiny bits of information to make a whole.

The Marchioness had been dark, with raven black hair and dark eyes which she had heard one of the footmen say "would make a man's heart stop beating in his breast with the expression in them".

What sort of expression could that mean? Gracila wondered.

She had puzzled over the elopement for so many years that now it seemed incredible that the whole drama and excitement of it was now connected with her own life.

The principal actor, young Romeo, as someone had described him scathingly, was here. She was actually sleeping in his house, although he was not aware of it.

"Whatever Mitty and Mrs. Hansell may say," Gracila murmured, "I have to catch a glimpse of him somehow, just to see if he is really like Lord Byron and decide for myself if he is as bad and as wicked as they all say he is."

She could hear her father's voice saying to her mother:

"That wicked young devil has broken his father's heart. What would we feel, Elizabeth, if a son of ours behaved in such a manner!"

There was a slight edge to the Earl's voice because it was a great sadness that although he had three sons by his first wife, Gracila was the only child of his second.

Gracila had had little contact with her half-brothers who were all married and had families of their own, and seldom came to the Castle.

The Earl had still been very young when they were born. They had never got on well with their father and had little interest in Gracila.

'Perhaps,' she thought now, 'what I need is a real brother I could turn to, who would support me in my decision that I cannot marry the Duke.'

She wondered if Lord Damien would understand, as her mythical brother would have done, her reasons for taking such a decisive step.

After all, he had run away from home, though for a very different reason!

"I suppose most people," Gracila ruminated to herself,

"would think it a cowardly thing to do."

Actually it had required a lot of courage.

There had been one moment while she was riding towards Barons' Hall on Caesar when her determination had wavered and she had almost gone back.

The five miles between the two houses had seemed a very long distance and though she had gone across the fields when darkness fell, she had suddenly felt that she was riding into the unknown.

'Surely, even if it was horrifying and shocking, the familiar was better?"

It was as if someone actually tempted her to go back and become a Duchess, to forget what she had overheard in the Library and pretend it had not happened.

Then she knew that perhaps that would have been possible with any woman other than her Step-mother. But in the case of someone who had taken her mother's place, who was married to her father, it was unthinkable!

It was then the sense of shock that Gracila had been experiencing swept over her so that she felt faint but a pride she had not known before seemed to rise up within her, almost like a torch of fire.

"I will not be weak over this!" she told herself. "I will not go back and I will not be afraid! What I am doing is right!"

She was right to be resolute and not be party to a loathsome intrigue! She was right not to lower her standards and ideals!

Now she knew that whatever happened in the future she would always be glad that she had not been cowardly enough to turn back.

It suddenly struck her as almost funny that Lord Damien, who was spoken of as being so wicked, so reprehensible in every possible way, should now, although he was supremely ignorant of it, be protecting her.

It was Lord Damien who would prevent her from being discovered and dragged back to face the music.

Because his reputation was so disgraceful, no-one would ever imagine that anyone so young and innocent as herself would be hiding in his house, let alone when he was actually in residence!

In the darkness of the Elizabethan room Gracila smiled as she thought how horrified all those chattering, gossiping friends of her Step-mother would be.

What a titbit it would be to repeat and re-repeat amongst themselves!

"Do you know where the lost bride has gone?" they would ask each other. "To Barons' Hall!"

"That must be Lord Damien's doing!"

"But how could she have met him?"

"Does that matter? She is there with him!"

"Are you saying that Gracila is actually staying at Barons' Hall? I always suspected that girl was not all she appeared to be!"

"Well, it is a good thing the poor Duke found out before she actually had his ring on her finger!"

"It will be quite easy for him to find another bride, but very unlikely that Gracila Shering will find a husband!"

There would be tinkling laughter at this and then some-one would say:

"There is one thing of which we can be certain, Lord Damien will not marry her! He has never married any of the dozens of women who have been in his life, so why should he start now?"

Gracila chuckled. It was almost like listening to a play!

Then she told herself that for her father's sake, if for no-one else's, no-one must ever know that she and Lord Damien were under the same roof!

Chapter Three

Gracila slipped out of a side door of the house and keeping in the shelter of the shrubs moved towards the stream at the lower end of the lake.

It was the first time she had dared to go outside since she had arrived at Barons' Hall.

With the fragrance of lilac and syringa scenting the air and the glimpses through the leaves of golden patches of late daffodils, she thought the garden had never looked lovelier.

In the two years since the late Lord Damien had died, it had become wild and over-grown.

The Trustees of the Estate, her father had told her, had decided to dispense with all the young servants and retain only those who had been in the Damien service for years and were due shortly to retire.

While Mrs. Hansell had managed to keep the house clean and very much the same as when her Master was alive, the gardeners had been unable to cope with Nature.

Now everything appeared to have become unrestrainedly luxuriant as if the very shrubs themselves rejoiced in being free and untrammelled.

The laburnums were just coming into bloom and the purple lilac made a great patch of colour against the first crimson buds of the rhododendrons.

It was so lovely that Gracila felt she wanted to dance like a nymph among the bushes and hold up her arms to the almond blossom, pink and white against the blue sky.

Could anywhere in the world be lovelier than May in England? She wondered if that was why Lord Damien had returned home.

Although they were living under the same roof, it was hard for her to learn anything about him. Whenever she asked questions, Mrs. Hansell answered her with pursed lips, and Millet did much the same.

"Tell me, Mitty, what is His Lordship having for dinner tonight?" Gracila had enquired yesterday evening when the old Butler had brought up her tray.

She had her meals in a small room next to her Bedroom which Mrs. Hansell had arranged as a Sitting-room.

Gracila knew, although she herself would not have minded at all, that Mrs. Hansell disapproved of the idea of her eating in her bedroom.

"It's much the same as you're having, M'Lady," Millet had answered.

Then he had changed the subject, clearly having no wish to speak of his new Master.

They were so obviously afraid that she might grow interested in Lord Damien, that she longed to tell them she had been interested in him ever since she had been a child.

Sooner or later, whatever they might say, she intended to see him.

It was, however, not easy.

Lord Damien slept in the Master-suite which was at the other end of the house, and there was nowhere that she could hide to peep at him walking down the main staircase, or moving through the big corridors in the Georgian part of the building.

"I shall just have to bide my time," Gracila told herself.

One thing was certain, she would get no help from Millet or Mrs. Hansell!

"I must go out, I must have some air," she had said to the latter yesterday.

She had been forced to sit in her Bedroom and Sitting-room all day and felt imprisoned because the sun was shining in through the windows.

"It's impossible, M'Lady," Mrs. Hansell had said firmly. "I've no idea where His Lordship may be and you knows as well as I do what would happen if he saw you!"

"What would happen?" Gracila asked curiously.

"It would mean, M'Lady, whatever you might say, you'd have to leave," Mrs. Hansell replied.

Gracila knew she was right. At the same time it was very much like being in the charge of a very severe Governess or, worse still, an over-protective Nanny.

Gracila was sure Mrs. Hansell thought her restlessness might lead her to do something regrettable, but she had said this morning when she called her:

"You'll be able to go out today, M'Lady."

"I can?" Gracila asked. "But how exciting! Why?"

"His Lordship has ordered a horse and I understand it's his intention to ride to the far boundary of the Estate."

"Wonderful!" Gracila exclaimed.

"Your Ladyship's aware that it'll take him several hours and his Valet informs us that he'll have luncheon out."

"That means I can spend the morning in the woods!" Gracila exclaimed. "You know how I love them at this time of the year."

Mrs. Hansell's face softened.

"I remember once, M'Lady — you couldn't have been more than five or six at the time — when I was avisiting Millet, you brought me some primroses you had picked yourself. You looked like them."

She smiled and went on:

"As I was asaying to Millet only last night, you've not altered."

"I have grown a little bigger, I hope?" Gracila asked.

"Your face's the same," Mrs. Hansell said, "just like your dear Lady-mother, who never seemed to age an' looked a child to her dying day."

"She was always beautiful," Gracila said in a low voice.

She thought Mrs. Hansell was going to pay her the compliment of saying she too looked beautiful, but instead the House-keeper fetched a gown from the wardrobe, to say briskly:

50

"I've prepared your bath, M'Lady, and put out one of your plainest gowns, though if you ask me they're all too grand for wandering about the garden and sitting on the grass as like as not!"

"I will be very careful," Gracila said meekly. "I have a feeling they will have to last me a very long time."

She did not wait for Mrs. Hansell's reply, but had her bath and ate an excellent breakfast in the small Sitting-room.

The sun was pouring in through the windows and she felt as excited at the thought that she could be outside as if she were going to a Ball.

Now, realising with delight that there was no hurry, she could enjoy everything around her, she stopped to touch the wax-like blossoms on a magnolia-tree with gentle fingers.

Magnolias always grew well at Barons' Hall and Gracila remembered how proud the late Lord Damien had been of his trees.

"Not many places in England where they flower as well as they do here," he would say every time anyone admired them.

To Gracila they personified the East which she had read about in books and of which she longed to know more.

Perhaps one day she would be able to travel to Egypt, Persia or India, countries that had a mysterious exotic allure about them, and, she was sure, a beauty as compelling and mystic as the magnolia blossom she was touching.

She walked on and at length came to the stream which flowed out of the lake. It was not very wide and twisted and turned through trees until, eventually passing through thick woods, it reached the boundary of the Damien Estate.

There were trout in the stream and as the water was clear she could see them swimming against the gravel bottom moving with a grace that made her envious.

'How lovely if I could swim like that,' she thought to herself.

She remembered how she had tried to do so when she was a child in the lake at the Castle.

But when she was ten years old she was told she was too old for bathing. Someone might see her.

"Who would be interested?" she had asked, "and would it matter if someone did?"

There was, as she knew, no answer to her question. Swimming was ruled out because a lady could not appear in open air, whether anyone saw her or not, unless she was fully clothed.

It was a bore growing up, Gracila had thought at the time, and she told herself now it was still a bore!

Why should she have to think of marriage and through no inclination of her own find herself involved in the present disastrous situation.

She had no wish to marry a Duke even though her Step-mother, entirely to suit her own ends, had made it sound so exciting.

'I was quite happy as I was!' Gracila thought resentfully. 'It was so nice not to have Governesses fussing round me. I enjoyed too the few parties I attended in London!'

Looking back she realised that the three weeks she had spent there ostensibly to buy clothes, had been curtailed simply because her Step-mother was putting into operation, the plan for her to marry the Duke.

"You can come back when the Season begins," she had said when Gracila, having made some new friends, had protested at returning home.

"When does the Season start?" she asked.

"In April," her Step-mother had replied briefly.

By April she was engaged to be married and although most girls had long engagements, Gracila was told that her marriage would take place on May 31st.

"What is the point of waiting," her Step-mother had

asked with unanswerable logic, "when you can appear at a Drawing-room at Buckingham Palace as a Duchess instead of my presenting you as a Débutante?"

It had sounded quite sensible. At the same time Gracila had the feeling, although she had not put it into words, that she was being rushed.

But now she was free! And she decided last night, as she lay awake in the quietness of the Elizabethan Room, she would not look too far ahead.

It was frightening to wonder what would happen to her.

Frightening to plan what she would do with no money and nowhere to go.

"Luck has been on my side so far," she told herself, "and what could be luckier than to have Mitty to help me!"

When she had run down a secondary staircase to a side-door which led into the garden, she felt as if she was a bird escaping from a cage.

She had not put on a bonnet, which she was sure Mrs. Hansell would have expected.

Instead she had just finished her breakfast and slipped away before anyone could stop her or give her instructions as to what she could or could not do.

She felt rather guilty, but at the same time for the moment she was her own mistress!

She bent down to dip her fingers in the clear water of the stream and watch the small fish scatter from her in alarm into the shadows.

There were violets on the bank, and a little further inside the wood there was the smell of pine and the scent of Spring.

It had, Gracila told herself, a very special fragrance, different from any other time of the year.

She walked on, keeping along the bank of the stream, until ahead of her the wood thickened and the sun could not penetrate the branches.

It looked mysterious and romantic but at the same time a little dark, and today Gracila wished to keep in the sunshine.

Slowly she retraced her steps to where the branches of the trees almost over-hung the stream on either side, making it appear as if the water passed through a green tunnel.

Here, without a thought of Mrs. Hansell's reproaches, Gracila sat down on the grass.

She picked a few violets within reach of her hands and put them in her lap and then she slipped away into the day-dreams that her Governesses had always found so reprehensible.

She was inventing a story that she told herself, in which she herself took part.

They were always happy stories, peopled not with human beings but with mythical gods and goddesses that she had read about in the books on mythology.

They were far more exciting than the friends she knew or even her own family, and with them were all the creatures of her fairy tales – nymphs and elves; goblins and fauns; witches and ogres.

It was an escape into a dream-land which swept away her worry, the incessant question as to what was happening at the Castle, and what her father and Step-mother had done when they found she had disappeared.

It must have been nearly two hours later that Gracila was suddenly aware that there was a new sound, different from the buzz of the bees, the cooing of the wood pigeons, and the rustle of small animals in the under-growth.

For a moment it only blended with the music of the rest.

Then she was aware that it was in fact the sound of horses' hooves and someone was approaching.

She sprang to her feet like a startled faun.

'No-one must find me here,' she thought and looked round for somewhere to hide.

If she ran towards the trees she thought her white dress might be seen, but where else could she go?

Then she saw she had been sitting beneath an ancient crab-apple tree and her experienced eye told her it would be easy to climb.

She had always been good at climbing.

In fact this had often provided for her an escape from Nanny or Governess ever since she had been small.

She used to drive them mad when they shouted and searched for her, only to find she had been within a few feet of them all the time hidden amongst the leaves of some tall tree.

It was easy now, thought Gracila, to lift up the skirt of her expensive gown with a quick thought of what Mrs. Hansell would say if she ruined it, and to climb up the rough trunk of the tree with, on the whole, very little damage done to her white lace-edged petticoats.

She climbed higher and higher until she found she could rest comfortably in a fork where it was unlikely the approaching rider would see her unless he deliberately looked up amongst the thick leaves.

She was only just in time because coming through the woods she now saw a horse and on it a man.

One glance at him was enough to make Gracila's heart leap, because she knew without being told, that she was seeing, as she had longed to do, Lord Damien himself!

At first he was too far away for her to see him clearly.

Then she could see that, like her, he was bare-headed, that his hair was dark and in the Byronic style swept back loosely from his forehead.

Even before she could see further the words came to her mind:

"Sun-burnt his cheek, his forehead high and pale
The sable curls in wild profusion veil."

She almost laughed aloud at how accurate the description was.

Then as the horse drew nearer she could see him more clearly and thought that he was everything that Lord Byron must have been!

Yet perhaps even more impressive, because there was an air of authority about him.

"And oft perforce his rising lip reveals
The haughtier thought it curbs, but scarce conceals ..."

He had a straight aristocratic nose, and his dark eyes were looking at the stream which was why, Gracila thought, he was riding so slowly.

He pulled his horse to a standstill, his face still turned sideways to stare down at the water.

'He is looking at the trout,' Gracila thought, 'exactly as I did.'

Now as she stared at his profile she could understand the way the women had spoken of him from her Stepmother and her friends down to the servants.

He was the handsomest man she had ever actually seen, apart from her imagination, and he looked, in fact, exactly as she had always imagined he would.

No wonder there were so many scandals attached to his name!

No wonder the Marchioness had run away with him, causing a commotion that after all these years still vibrated through the County.

No wonder he had been a success in Paris, Venice, Rome, Naples and Palermo! Who could resist beauty wherever it might be found?

Lord Damien was now moving on.

Gracila realised that he would pass directly beneath the bough on which she was hiding, and as he was on horseback his head would pass really quite close beneath her.

She drew in her breath, wishing that she had not chosen this particular tree but had moved away from the stream before she climbed to safety.

He had reached her tree and had to bend his head so that the branches would not brush his face.

As he did so there was a sudden flash of brilliant colour in the stream beside him, which made him once again draw in his horse.

It was a kingfisher that attracted his attention, which Gracila had glimpsed once or twice while she had been sitting still on the grass.

Now, because of its lovely meteoric movement, Lord Damien had stopped close below her and she could, if she had reached down her arm have touched the top of his head.

He was wearing riding-breeches, a cut-away coat and, she saw almost incredulously, an open-necked Byronic shirt which had become the fashion a few years earlier.

Gracila could remember her father denouncing it as an effete, slovenly and an ungentlemanly fashion.

She tried to remember who had told her, and thought it must have been her Step-mother, that Prince Albert had worn one the morning after his wedding, in order to dazzle Queen Victoria.

"I do not believe it!" the Earl had said sharply, "and even if it is true, no gentleman sits down at my table unless he is decently dressed!"

It certainly made Lord Damien look poetical, and yet at the same time there was something about him which denied that appearance.

It was, however, difficult to think coherently and critically when he was so near her.

Then there being no further sight of the kingfisher, he lifted his hand which was holding the reins preparatory to moving on. As he did so he looked up.

It must have been an instinctive feeling of someone's presence or perhaps the intensity of Gracila's scrutiny communicated it to him.

Whatever it was, he looked up into the branch over his head and saw between the leaves a small oval face looking down at him and two vividly blue eyes.

The horse had already begun to step forward when it was pulled sharply to a stand-still.

Lord Damien's face remained upturned and there was a perceptible silence before he asked:

"May I enquire if you are Daphne fleeing from Apollo, or a runaway young star?"

His voice was deep and had an amused note in it.

For a moment Gracila was so surprised he had seen her and was speaking to her that she found it impossible to reply.

Then because it was in keeping with his appearance that he should quote from one of her favourite poems, she answered:

"Well ... the angels were ... singing out of ... tune!"

Lord Damien laughed.

"So you know your Byron!"

His horse fidgeted and was held in check.

"Come down," Lord Damien said, "unless you are in a hurry to return to the sky from which you have fallen!"

For a moment Gracila hesitated.

Such a meeting was just what she had been ordered to avoid, but there seemed no point, when he had found her, in refusing to speak to him.

They could hardly go on talking as they were, with his head upturned and she clinging to a bough.

He was obviously waiting for her answer and after a moment she said:

"Very well ... but ride on a ... little way."

"Why?"

She smiled and he saw she had a dimple on either side of her mouth.

"It is not particularly decorous to climb trees, and even less so when one descends them!"

Lord Damien laughed again and then he said:

"You will come and talk to me. You won't disappear so that I have to hunt you through the sky?"

"No, I will talk to you," Gracila promised.

He moved on, brushing through the branches, then drew his horse to a halt.

He swung himself to the ground and as he did so

Gracila climbed down the tree, hoping he would not look back to see the most unladylike exposure of silk stocking.

She was careful once again with her gown, but when she reached the ground there were quite a number of green stains on her petticoats.

She put up her hands in an instinctive gesture to her hair, then walked through the trees to where Lord Damien was waiting for her beside the stream.

He was taller than she had expected and far more broad-shouldered.

Despite the open-neck shirt he did not look so poetical as she had anticipated, in fact very masculine, and rather older than she had thought he would be.

There was definitely an expression of surprise on his face and his eye-brows were raised as he said :

"I imagined you were a child. I see I was mistaken."

There was something in the tone with which he spoke which made Gracila blush.

"It would certainly be ... better," she said, "if you continue to ... think of me as a ... child, or, if you prefer, a ... runaway star!"

"Why?"

"There are reasons."

"The most obvious, I suppose, being that you should not be talking to me!"

Now his face changed and there was no mistaking the cynical, almost bitter note in it.

Gracila looked at him sharply.

Now she knew why she thought his appearance was not poetic.

Now she knew why he looked older.

"But I want to talk to you," Lord Damien went on. "I like mysteries, and I cannot remember ever before finding a star hidden in a tree, and certainly not in one of my trees!"

"It would really be ... best if you ... forgot you have ... seen me," Gracila said hesitatingly.

"That is quite an absurd suggestion and, as I have no

wish to gallop after you, may I beg you to sit down and talk to me."

As if she surrendered, not to him, but to the inevitable, Gracila made a little gesture of her hands.

"You leave me little . . . alternative."

Lord Damien looked round and she realised he was wondering where he could tie up his horse.

"Sampson will not wander," she said, "and if he does, it will be easy for you to catch him."

"So you know the name of my horse!"

Gracila realised she had spoken without thinking.

Sampson was an old horse. Most of those in the Stables were, and she had fed him dozens of times on her visits to Barons' Hall.

This was why she knew that he was very unlikely to go home on his own as a younger animal might have done.

As if he trusted what she had said, Lord Damien knotted the reins on Sampson's neck and turned round to say:

"Shall we sit by the stream? I saw a kingfisher just now."

"A pair nest here every year."

"Tell me about them," Lord Damien said, "and other things you know about my property."

As he spoke he chose a place where the grass was short and apparently dry. It was sheltered by trees but the sun was on the water in front of them.

Gracila sat down, her back straight, her eyes wide and undisguisedly curious as she looked at Lord Damien.

He stretched himself beside her and she realised that while he was graceful he was undeniably strong and athletic. Not, she thought, like a poet or a debauchee weakened by riotous living.

He rested his head on his arm and looked up at her to say:

"Now tell me about yourself."

"That is . . . something unfortunately I cannot . . . do."

"Why not?"

"There are very good reasons ... but they are ... secret."

"Are you being deliberately provocative?" he enquired. She shook her head.

"I am telling you the truth. I suppose ... really I am ... asking you to ... help me."

"To help you? How can I do that?"

"By not being too ... inquisitive."

"Perhaps that is what you mean me to be!"

"I was ... hiding from ... you."

"But why?"

She hesitated and then before she could answer he said harshly:

"There is no need to answer that question! You are hiding from me as any sensible and well-behaved woman would be told to do!"

Again there was so much bitterness in his voice that instinctively Gracila put out her hand as if to reassure him. Then she dropped it in her lap.

"I was not ... hiding for that ... reason," she said. "Well, ... not ... exactly."

"That is not very informative," Lord Damien remarked.

"I know," Gracila replied, "but it is ... difficult."

"It is you who are difficult. I find you hidden in a tree, and you say you are hiding from me – but not exactly!"

"It would have been far ... better if you had ... ridden on."

"But not half so interesting!" he retorted, and because Gracila could not help it, she laughed.

He watched her. Then he said:

"I thought you were a child, but now I see you closely, I find you are one of the most beautiful women I have ever seen, and yet – not yet a woman."

The colour rose in Gracila's cheeks and she looked away from him across the stream.

"There are a hundred questions I want to ask you," Lord Damien said. "Who are you? Why are you here?

Why are you so mysterious? But first I just want to say that I find it a privilege to look at you and I think perhaps I am dreaming!"

"Dreaming," Gracila murmured.

"That anything so lovely, so unexpected, so perfect in its own way, should be at Barons' Hall."

Again there was a harsh note in his voice and Gracila said:

"Do not speak of it like that. Can you not see how beautiful it is, especially in May? That I thought might be the reason why you have come home."

> "Shall I compare thee to a Summer's day?
> Thou art more lovely and more temperate.
> Rough winds do shake the darling buds of May."

He quoted the lines softly with his eyes on Gracila's face. Then as she did not speak, he said:

"Actually my reason for returning was a desire for sanctuary."

"Sanctuary!" Gracila exclaimed in surprise.

"It is something I do not wish to discuss," Lord Damien said quickly. "Instead I want to talk about you."

"And that is something I do not wish to discuss!"

"Then what shall we talk about?" he asked. "It is not a question I would have to ask most women, but I think, my little star, that you are very young in fact

> "A lovely being, scarcely form'd or moulded,
> A rose with all its sweetest leaves yet folded."

Gracila smiled at the quotation and after a moment he said:

"Now tell me, why should anyone as young and beautiful as you be hiding?"

Gracila thought for a moment before she said:

"If I tell you a ... little ... just to assuage your ... curiosity, will you promise me ... something?"

"Most promises are dangerous!"

"It would not be dangerous for you to give it, but if you ... broke it, it would be dangerous for ... me."

"Then of course I give you my promise."

"Then will you swear that you will not mention to anyone that you have seen me ... or that we have talked ... together?"

He raised his eye-brows.

"I am alone."

He paused, then added:

"You mean the servants?"

Gracila nodded.

"You are telling me that they are privileged to know what you will not tell me?"

"Not ... exactly," Gracila answered, "but if you tell Millet ..."

"My Butler?"

"Yes, Millet. If you tell him you have seen me, or Mrs. Hansell, your House-keeper, then they will send me away."

"You mean you are staying in my house? In Barons' Hall?"

"I have ... nowhere else to ... go."

"I am extremely honoured and delighted you should be my guest, but will you tell me why there was nowhere else to go?"

He glanced as he spoke at her gown, and she thought that he was well aware that it was an extremely expensive one.

Poverty was not the reason, then what could it be?

She knew he was waiting and after a moment she said hesitatingly:

"I ... I ... was ... involved in a very ... uncomfortable and ... difficult ... situation ... from which I had ... to ... escape."

"What you are saying, is that you have had to run away?"

"Yes"

"No wonder I thought you were a runaway star! Were you surprised that I quoted Byron?"

"I somehow ... expected it. I have always ... connected you in my mind with ... Lord Byron."

"So you have known about me and thought about me. It is not fair!"

"What is not fair?"

"That you should know about me and I know nothing about you except that you do in fact look like a small runaway star, that has fallen out of Heaven to bemuse a mere man."

Gracila laughed.

"That has always been one of my favourite passages because it makes me laugh when I feel depressed or ... unhappy."

It struck her it was what she had been reading when her Step-mother and the Duke had come into the Library.

Lord Damien watched her face and after a moment he said quietly:

"You have been hurt and shocked. What could have caused that?"

"How ... do you ... know?"

Both her eyes and her voice were startled.

"Your eyes are very revealing," he said. "I can see what you are thinking even though you are determined you will not tell me the truth with your lips!"

"What you have ... said is ... true," she said in a low voice. "I was shocked by ... something which ... happened and so I ... ran away to Barons' Hall."

"But why in God's name to Barons' Hall?"

The dimples were back in her cheeks as Gracila replied:

"I knew it was the last place where anyone would look for me!"

For a moment Lord Damien stared at her. Then he laughed.

"Now I understand," he exclaimed, "and I find it a rare jest and one that I appreciate. Just as I have sought sanctuary in my home you have done the same thing."

"You will keep your promise?" Gracila pleaded. "Otherwise it will no longer be a sanctuary and I shall ... have to ... leave."

"Do you think I would really hurt you, or do anything to distress you?" he asked. "It would be a crime against Heaven itself!"

There was something in the way he spoke that made her feel shy.

"Trust me further," he begged, "or shall we wait until we know each other better?"

"It would be quite ... wrong to suggest that we ... should get to know each other at all."

"Why should it be wrong?" he asked, "especially if no-one knows!"

"But we might be ... found out. We might be ... seen."

"Then we must take care we are not."

"That would be difficult," she answered, "and it would in fact be far ... easier for us to keep our ... sanctuaries in different parts of the ... house and not ... meet."

"That would not only be intolerable, but extremely dull," Lord Damien said positively. "I was already feeling depressed with my own thoughts, oppressed by the solitude and ..."

He smiled before he finished:

"I really think you have been sent like a star to bring me light."

"It seems strange that you should be ... distressed or ... unhappy," Gracila said in a low voice.

"Why strange?"

"Because everyone has always talked about you being immersed in gaiety; giving parties surrounded by beautiful women ..."

She stopped because she saw the expression on Lord Damien's face.

"I ... am sorry," she said after a second, "if ... I have said anything to upset ... you."

"You have only said what I expected to hear, and unfortunately it is irrefutably true."

"Then why ... why does it make you ... unhappy?"

She thought he was searching for words before he said:

"Happiness is perhaps too much to ask of life, but some people, especially those like you and me, need security."

"You are right! Of course you are right!" Gracila cried. "I wanted to feel ... safe which was why I came to Barons' Hall."

"And I came because it is mine; because it is the only place to which I really belong; the only roots I have!"

There was something savage in the way he spoke.

She thought that the violence of his feelings seemed to contort his face and once again he looked older than he was.

"And now you are home," she asked after a moment, "does everything feel better?"

"How can it ever be better?" he asked. "And to me it is not really a home – rather an empty shell. I have no home, I am a wanderer on the face of the earth, a man who needs safety and security and can find neither!"

Again there was silence until Gracila said:

"I understand ... what you are ... saying and perhaps a ... little of what you are ... feeling. But surely, if the ... reason you have not come home before is what ... happened a very long ... time ago, you are ... exaggerating it!"

"Can you really suggest I am exaggerating," Lord Damien asked, "when you have just said yourself that if it was known that we were meeting like this, you would have to leave?"

He asked the question sharply. Then to his surprise Gracila smiled and her eyes twinkled.

"Where your presence here concerns me," she answered, "is because of what might happen in the ... future, not because of the ... past!"

"That is not true," he answered. "You are afraid for

yourself, or rather those who are looking after you are afraid because of my reputation and my behaviour in the past."

"I think their reaction would be very much the same, whatever you had done or not done," Gracila said. "After all, for a young unmarried girl to stay alone under the same roof as a gentleman would be reprehensible, even if he was blind, deaf and dumb!"

"Thank God I am none of those things!" Lord Damien replied. "At the same time I am a roué, a rake, a man with no morals, a debauchee and a reprobate!"

The words rolled from his lips and again Gracila laughed.

"So you know they said all those things about you!"

"Of course!"

"And how they have enjoyed saying them!" she said. "Ever since I was a child I have heard them talking about you and listened to the excitement in their voices!"

She paused for a moment before she added:

"It is difficult to put into words, but you have brought a kind of ... vicarious joy of ... living to so many people that I cannot think your ... behaviour ... whatever it may have been ... is entirely ... reprehensible!"

Lord Damien looked at her and then as if he could not help himself, he laughed:

"Did you really think that out yourself, or did someone say it to you?"

"You forget I am not supposed to talk about you, let alone talk with you!"

He laughed again. Then he said:

"How could I have imagined there was anyone like you in the whole world? If I listen to you long enough, all the bogeys will fly away and I might believe after all that there was joy in Heaven."

"Have you repented for your bad deeds?"

"It is not so much a question of repentance," he replied, "but of utter boredom."

"Oh! no!"

"Why do you say it like that?"

"Because it would be such a waste! You have been away for twelve years. You must have ... enjoyed what you were ... doing for all that ... long time."

There was a somewhat twisted smile on his lips as he said:

"You are trying to tell me that 'sin is a pleasure'. Some of it undoubtedly was, but anything, however delectable, can become stale. Then one begins to criticise, to regret, and it eats into one's soul."

He spoke with a despondency which suddenly made her angry.

"How can you be so absurd as to think of it like that?" she asked. "In fact, I cannot believe you are serious!"

"About what?"

"About your life. That is what you are talking about. You are complaining that everything you have done has turned sour, and so you are ... mourning the past instead of looking ... forward to the ... future!"

"What is there to look forward to?"

Gracila sighed.

"There are so many things to do, to see, to hear, to appreciate. How can you let anything or anybody spoil that?"

"As I have already said," Lord Damien answered, "you are very young. When I was young I felt as you did, but now I am getting old."

"You are thirty-one!" Gracila said. "Not yet even in what they call the 'prime of life'! And you think yourself an old man! Well, I am sorry for you, but now I think I ought to go."

She would have risen to her feet but Lord Damien put out his hand.

"Do not dare to leave me! There is so much more I have to say to you. So much we have to discuss, perhaps quarrel about, and I will make you stay even if I have to do so forcibly!"

"That is unfair," Gracila retorted. "You know that, whatever you do, I may not cry out for help. I cannot even tell Millet I have met you."

"Or," he added, "that I have behaved in exactly the way everyone would have expected me to do!"

"I do not ... think that is ... true."

"Why?"

She looked at him and then she said slowly:

"I have a feeling that you, like many other people, are making yourself out to be much worse than you really are. Will you ... believe me if I say that I ... trust you?"

"I believe you," he replied, "but it is very stupid of you!"

Gracila smiled.

"I do not think so. I am always right in knowing when I can trust someone. I know I can trust you."

His lips tightened before he said:

"You are undermining the only thing I was sure about, my own wickedness!"

"I am sorry if it disappoints you," Gracila said, "but because I ... like talking to you ... because I find it very ... exciting and ... interesting, it is easier to tell you the truth. I do ... trust you."

Their eyes met and they looked at each other for a long moment. Then he said:

"I was right! You are not human, you are different from anyone I have ever met before."

"And so are you!" she answered. "But there is no logical conclusion to be drawn from that!"

He laughed.

"God knows how you have been brought up or why, looking as you do, you need to be intelligent! Now tell me about yourself."

"Tell me first, what is the time?" Gracila replied.

Lord Damien looked surprised but he drew a gold watch from the pocket of his waist-coat.

"It is nearly a quarter to one o'clock."

Gracila gave a little cry.

"I must go back! They will wonder what has ... happened to me and it might be difficult for me to come into the garden another day."

"What do you mean? I do not understand?"

She smiled at him.

"It is quite simple. Millet and Mrs. Hansell are determined I shall not meet you. Therefore I was told this morning that you were riding to the boundary of the Estate and would be out for luncheon."

"That is what I intended to do," Lord Damien said, "but it was hot and I suddenly thought I had no wish to eat bread and cheese in a local Inn but to come home. If nothing else, the food is good at Barons' Hall."

Gracila had a feeling that the truth was he had funked causing the curiosity and excitement his presence would have been bound to evoke at any Inn on the Estate.

"If we arrive back almost at the ... same time," she said, "Millet will be so ... nervous that we might have met that he and Mrs. Hansell will make a terrible commotion the next time I want to come ... here or ... anywhere else."

Lord Damien smiled.

"I understand. I will go hungry and stay away until later in the afternoon. Will that please you?"

Gracila smiled and then dropping her eyes a little shyly she said in a low voice:

"If Your Lordship is not ... returning until ... late I can have my luncheon and ... come back here."

"What a surprise if I should ride back this way, or perhaps I will just wait for your return."

"I would not ... like to think of you as ... hungry."

"It is good for the soul to fast."

"You seem very preoccupied with your soul," she teased, "or is it your ... heart that is causing the most ... trouble?"

"I do not believe after all that you have dropped from

the Heavens," he replied, "but are an abominable brat sent to torment me!"

"In which case I can only withdraw with dignity," Gracila replied.

She rose as she spoke and Lord Damien did the same.

For a moment they stood looking at each other and Gracila felt her heart was beating in a way it had never done before.

Then Lord Damien said:

"If I wait for you here, do you swear you will come back?"

She could not find her voice to reply and he added:

"If you do not, I will take the house down brick by brick to find you and cross-examine everyone in it!"

"You gave me your promise!" she protested.

"And I will keep it if you will keep yours to return here as soon as you have finished your luncheon."

"I will come," she answered, "but now I must... hurry."

She turned away but Lord Damien said quickly:

"You have not yet told me your name. I must have a name by which to think of you."

"Gracila," she replied, and wondered as she started running through the trees if she had been indiscreet.

It was an unusual name and it might be easy for him to discover who she was.

Then she told herself that having given his promise there was no one he would question, he would keep it.

Besides which, as she had only been six years old when he left England there was nothing to connect her with any of his neighbours, if he still remembered them.

As she sped towards the house Gracila told herself that meeting Lord Damien was the most exciting, adventurous thing she had ever done.

He was different, so different from what she had ever expected, and yet in a way it was inevitable that the pictures other people had painted of him would be false.

"It is false," Gracila said in her mind, "if they believe he is bad and wicked. He is neither of these things but he is disillusioned."

It struck her that she had discovered the meaning of the expression on his face which had puzzled her.

It was disillusionment!

Chapter Four

Lord Damien looked round the large Library in which his father had always sat.

It had been started in 1700 and the ceiling, with its gilded plaster work and circular panels, had been painted by Verrio.

He remembered how as a child he had loved running along the balcony round the upper half of the room and down the twisting staircase which stood in a corner.

He had not then appreciated the magnificent gilt, carved pelmets or the furniture which, like the mahogany writing table designed by William Kent, made the room unique.

But now he was not really admiring its perfect proportions, or the goddesses rioting on the ceiling. Instead he was hearing his father's voice say:

"This cannot go on, Virgil. You are getting talked about and you know as well as I do, the Marchioness is too important in the County for there to be any scandal connected with her!"

He had not answered and after a moment his father said sternly:

"You will not see her any more. That is an order! Do you understand? If not, I will send you away!"

It was a threat which he had known his father would put into practice if he did not obey, but at that moment he had known what he must do, and that no-one could stop him.

On his journey back to England he had been aware that everything he saw would bring back memories that would be like a knife twisting in an open wound.

But he had suddenly decided he could stay away no longer and he had walked out of a riotous party taking place in Paris amidst cries of protest from the other guests.

It had all started over some absurd remark which, because he was in one of his black moods, he had taken as an insult.

He had known by the expression on the face of the man with whom he was arguing that if he continued it would end in yet another duel.

God knew he had fought too many since the first one in which he had been engaged and to contemplate another was to bring back the agony that he had suffered then.

As he had expected, Barons' Hall was full of ghosts – of his father ordering him about as if he were a child not old enough to understand and too young to resent it, of his mother, of himself.

Also, as might have been expected, the gardens, the woods, the very scent of the flowers recalled Phenice.

Heavens, what a fool he had been, so gullible, so absurdly idealistic! How was he to know that the ideal he worshipped would have feet of clay!

He remembered the first time he had ever seen her.

"I want you to come with me this afternoon," his father had said, in this very room, "to call on the new Marchioness of Lynmouth. After all the Marquess is one of my oldest friends and I feel extremely remiss that he has now been married for three months and I have not yet paid his wife my respects."

"Must we really waste the afternoon?" Virgil had asked.

He had planned to go fishing, and the idea of having to dress up and accompany his father in a closed carriage was annoying when he had so many better things to do.

"It is only polite, Virgil," Lord Damien had insisted, "and we need not stay long."

He had remembered that if his mother were alive she would have gone with his father and, knowing how lonely he must be without her, he agreed without further argument and went upstairs to change his clothes.

The Marquess's Estate bordered theirs and there were ways, which he was to know very well later, which shortened the distance considerably.

As it was, they had to proceed down the two-mile drive of Barons' Hall, through the Village and up the even longer drive which led to Lynmouth House.

It was an extremely ugly Mansion, built by an Architect who was obsessed by size rather than style. Virgil had thought, as they approached it, that it rather resembled its owner in having dignity without grace!

He was aware that the Marquess had been widowed for some years. He was a spokesman in the House of Lords and respected by the Government for his knowledge of Foreign Affairs.

It had been on a visit to Paris, where he was representing the Prime Minister, that he had met his present wife.

Virgil had not been particularly interested.

He knew that the Marquess was older than his father and he was quite certain that any woman he married would not enliven what he had begun to think of as a dull neighbourhood.

At Oxford he was enjoying all the gaiety and irresponsible high spirits of his undergraduate friends.

A Member of the hard-drinking, hard-riding Bullingdon Club, he had already been involved in a number of pranks which had been frowned upon by the Authorities, but laughed off by the undergraduates.

He was also, however, intelligent enough to appreciate the exceptional facilities which made the University without equal in the whole world.

Perhaps his intellectual gifts were inherited from his paternal ancestors, but the poetical side of his nature, which contrasted strangely with his athletic prowess, was undoubtedly inherited from his mother's gentle and imaginative nature and the Irish blood in her veins.

Lady Damien had died when her son was quite young but she had left him as a legacy a spiritual sensitivity which made him very different from most of his contemporaries.

He had always been slightly ashamed of the feelings that were evoked in him by music and poetry, but at Oxford he had found kindred spirits.

They exchanged their views and were, he found, as expert in this field as his other friends who concentrated on horses and inevitably women!

The inside of Lynmouth House was as dull as its exterior.

The large heavy dark furniture against the dark walls made it a place without colour and a feeling of being shut out from the sunshine and the sky.

The Marquess greeted them with geniality. He was extremely fond of Lord Damien and had known Virgil since he was born.

"I was just about to write to you," he said to Lord Damien, "and ask you to dine with us. But my wife has been very tired since we arrived in England and has not felt like entertaining."

"A decision which depends on whom I have to entertain," a voice from the doorway remarked and they turned round as the Marchioness came into the room.

She was such a surprise that Virgil could only stare at her, forgetting his manners; forgetting everything except that she was the most beautiful, exciting and unusual woman he had ever seen.

Afterwards, even when she lived with him, he was never certain of her nationality. Ostensibly she was French, having married the Comte de Castigone who had been killed in a duel.

How well in later years Virgil was to know those duels and the danger of them!

Before marriage, her origins were obscure. She spoke warmly of her Greek mother, but Virgil came to suspect that somewhere hidden away in a long line of ancestors there was a touch of Moorish blood.

Undoubtedly her grandfather and his father before him had held important posts in French Algiers.

But whoever was accountable for this exquisite creature, one could only admire the slender, supple body which moved as sinuously as a snake.

Her huge, dark eyes seemed to fill her whole face so it was impossible to recall what other features she had.

As Virgil had looked into them he knew that he was lost, like a diver going deep down into the very depths of the ocean without a possibility of being able to return.

He was unable to move or speak but just stood staring, and she turned to the Marquess to ask:

"Why did you not tell me that Apollo lived next door? You know I am home-sick for the Isles of Greece!"

"Y . you like B . Byron?"

"But, of course," she replied softly. "We must read him together."

And after that it was Phenice! Phenice! Phenice!

He would not have dared to approach her if she had not come to him, calling the next day at Barons' Hall with a formal note from the Marquess asking them both to dine.

It was quite unnecessary for her to bring it in person as the engagement had been made before they left Lynmouth House and a groom could quite easily have carried it between the two houses.

But Phenice had come in style, her high-crowned bonnet with its veil-edge framing her face, her emerald green pelisse accentuating the darkness of her eyes.

It happened that Virgil was alone in the Library, his father having gone out by an open window into the garden to speak to one of the gardeners.

They had practically closed the Salons after his

mother's death, and when the servant announced 'The Marchioness of Lynmouth,' he had started to his feet thinking he could not have heard aright.

And yet she was there, moving towards him, her eyes looking up into his; her red mouth curving in a manner that seemed to mesmerise him.

"You are reading?" she enquired, seeing he held a book in his hand. "I do hope I have not interrupted you!"

"No! No! Of course – not. You are very – welcome. Will you please sit down, my father will not be long."

"Do not let us hurry him!"

She spoke softly with a beguiling note that had ensnared far more experienced men than an Oxford undergraduate.

"I am only just beginning to realise," she said in a low voice, "how lovely England is at this time of the year."

"You have not been to England before?"

"Only to London. But now I find I have so much to discover, so much to explore."

"Would you – allow me? Would you – permit me to show you the lake, the woods – the park?"

He tried wildly to think of other things that would interest her.

Her eyes held his.

"Would you really do that? It would not be a bore and take up too much of your time?"

There was nothing else that he had the slightest interest in doing except talk to this lovely creature and show her anything she wished to see.

They had met every day.

It was the Summer vacation, the weather was hot and dry and the Marquess was preoccupied with the County Show, the Archery Competition, a Review of the Yeomanry.

He also had constant messages from the Foreign Office which necessitated his going to London to give his opinion on certain aspects of the European situation.

"You are so kind to me," Phenice said to Virgil. "I should be lonely and unhappy, a stranger in a strange land, if you were not here."

"It is a privilege – an honour to be – with you."

Inevitably the whole poetical side of his nature awoke to her beauty and her charm.

She became in his mind Aphrodite, Helen of Troy, Cleopatra and all women to whom Lord Byron had written his poems.

"She walks in beauty, like the night!"
"There be none of Beauty's daughters with a magic like thee."

Magic! That was what Phenice brought him. A magic that swept him away on a crescendo of celestial music to fill his imagination with dreams of her.

He wanted to kneel at her feet; he longed to perform great deeds of valour; to save and protect her. He was ready to die for her if that was required of him.

He would have no more thought of touching her, or attempting to kiss her, than of laughing at anything sacred or holy.

She was not at that time in his mind human, but divine! He put her in a shrine in his heart and worshipped her.

When first she had given him her hand to hold as they walked together in the peace and quietness of the woods, he could hardly believe that the feelings of excitement and wonder which surged through him were not an insult.

Then finally on a moonlit night, when they left a party of elderly card-players to wander into the gardens, he found she was all woman.

He could not afterwards remember if he had put his arms round her, or whether she had pressed herself against him.

But her head had fallen back against his shoulder while her lips were raised to his invitingly.

All he knew was that when he kissed her it did not

seem real, it was as if one of the goddesses painted by Verrio had stepped down from the ceiling.

It was not so much love he felt for her as adoration and it was only later he told himself savagely he had been ensnared, mesmerised, hypnotised like a rabbit by a snake.

She told him of her loneliness, her unhappiness, and that her marriage had been a mistake.

Virgil was to learn that the Marquess had been as easily captivated as he had been by a woman who wanted a social position and money.

It was, however, typical of Phenice, or perhaps the strange conflicting mixture of her blood, that in having obtained what she wanted it ceased to have any value.

She had thought to be an English Marchioness, to be accepted at Court, to have a hereditary post of honour to the Queen of William IV would be everything she desired of life.

It certainly had made her friends in Paris green with envy, but Paris was far away and Phenice had never really been interested in women.

It was men she craved; men who, once she looked at them, could never escape; men to excite her and make her feel!

"Make love to me, Virgil," she would demand. "Make me feel! Feel – before I am too old for anything but boredom!"

It was in the Christmas vacation that Virgil became Phenice's lover.

He had received an urgent message to dine at Lynmouth House. His father was included in the invitation, but Lord Damien had, in fact, as most people in the County knew, been confined to the house for two weeks with both gout and bronchitis.

"Do you mind me leaving you, Father?" Virgil asked.

"No, of course not, my boy. Go and enjoy yourself. Tell the Marquess to come over and see me tomorrow. I feel well enough for visitors, though the Marquess can hardly be counted as one. I want to talk to him about that fence on the boundary."

"Very well, Father."

He tried to keep the eagerness out of his voice.

He had found it almost impossible to work during the Michaelmas term. His Tutors had asked him what was the matter and why he seemed to have lost the enthusiasm they had appreciated previously.

He could hardly tell them that he could not see the pages of the books he was reading because they were obscured by the image of Phenice's face and Phenice's eyes!

He wandered about all day thinking of her. At night he dreamt of her.

He had written and told her when he was returning home; a formal, polite, rather stiff letter, expecting it might be read by the Marquess.

Virgil knew very little of how a husband and wife behaved with each other.

He only knew that his mother had adored his father and they had been very happy. But how could he compare Phenice with his mother or any other woman he had known?

"What is the matter with you, Virgil?" his friends had asked at Oxford. "There are some jolly pretty actresses at the Play-House this week and we are giving a party. You will enjoy it!"

But Virgil did not enjoy the party. In fact his friends complained it was obvious his thoughts were elsewhere and his attitude put a damper on everything.

"Are those creatures," Virgil asked himself, "with their painted faces, their affected voices and their bold glances really women as Phenice is a woman?"

They made him feel sick and somehow, compared with Phenice, defamed the very name of womanhood!

He expected to find a party at Lynmouth House, but when he arrived and handed his cape and hat to a flunkey, he was to his surprise taken up the stairs.

"Her Ladyship's in her Boudoir, Sir," the Butler explained.

Virgil's heart was beating tumultuously as he walked down a corridor and a door was opened.

The room was dimly lit and scented with a strange, subtle Eastern perfume he did not recognise.

Phenice was lying on a *chaise-longue* wearing a diaphanous gown which revealed rather than concealed her exquisite figure.

She held out her hands to him.

He wanted to kneel down beside her and tell her how much he had missed her; how he had longed to see her; how she filled his thoughts!

But first there was dinner.

It was nothing like the well-cooked but dull English fare he had always eaten before at Lynmouth House. But he thought that in Phenice's presence any food would taste like ambrosia and any wine like nectar.

He found in fact it hard to eat, but his glass was replenished again and again.

He was hardly aware of what he said of what they talked about before the meal was finished and the servants withdrew leaving them alone.

"Phenice!"

His voice was like the cry of a drowning man. Then she was in his arms and he was kissing her wildly, insistently, passionately.

The separation of what had seemed like centuries accentuated his longing for her during the term at Oxford.

Afterwards he could never remember the actual moment when they moved from the Boudoir into the Bedroom and he had found himself in the great canopied bed with its scented sheets.

He was conscious of the beauty of Phenice in the flickering light from the fire; the fire which not only lit the room, but seemed to burst within him so that his

82

whole body became a volcano, raging, consuming, destroying thought.

There was only feeling and feeling was what Phenice had craved!

        *   *   *

How madly she had aroused him and yet while his voice was numb his whole body vibrated to the movement of her body, the hunger of her lips and the inflammatory passion in her words.

"Phenice! Phenice!"

The night repeated and repeated her name as did the sound of the wheels and the clip-clop of the horses' hooves as he drove home.

"Can it be true?" he asked himself the next morning, "that this perfect, this marvellous, this sacred woman has given herself to me?"

He wanted to go down on his knees and thank God that he had been so blessed.

He quoted Byron over and over again: *"I knew it was love, and I felt it was glory!"*

It was not easy to find opportunities when they could be together again. The Marquess returned, it was too cold to wander in the woods, and anyhow Phenice hated the cold.

Somehow they contrived to be alone, though courting danger every time they did so.

Even if emotionally unsatisfied, it was always an adventure so that Virgil thought of himself as Jason seeking the Golden Fleece: Ulysses sailing into the unknown; St. George killing a dragon; and most often as Sir Galahad seeking the Holy Grail.

It was Phenice who finally suggested that they should run away together.

He had hardly credited what she was saying. It had never struck him that he could ever call this wonderful woman his own.

He had only wanted to adore her and do what she

wished, and he had demanded nothing as his right.

"How c . could we d . do such a th . thing?" he stammered.

"I want you! I want to be with you!" Phenice replied. "I hate this house, I hate the cold and I hate – yes I – hate Edward!"

The words were out, and somehow Virgil was shocked because they had been said.

Phenice hated her husband, the man whose name she bore! It had somehow never struck him, in his preoccupation with her, to be jealous of the man to whom she was married.

"I believe Edward is suspicious," Phenice said. "Soon we shall be forbidden to see each other and that is something I could not bear!"

"But how can we go away? And where can we go?"

She had flung wide her arms.

"The world is ours! Think of Venice, of drifting on the Grand Canal in your arms! To be together in the sunshine in Rome! To cross the Mediterranean! Why not? Always in search of the sun!"

"But – how – how can we leave here. How could you desert the Marquess and your position?"

"My position!" Phenice shrugged her shoulders. "What does it mean but talking to a lot of boring and antiquated men and women. I want to be with you, Virgil! You make me feel as I have never felt before! I want the fire that you awake in me!"

Her voice vibrated and she shivered.

"Here in England it is so dull, so cold. I want to go away! Take me, Virgil. Please take me away!"

His head was in a whirl, it was impossible to think. Ideas and plans would not come to him.

He wanted to please her, to do what she wished, but how? How?

He had gone back home and his father had told him to give her up and not to see her any more!

Now Virgil looked round the Library.

Why had he not listened? Why had he not understood that his father was speaking for his own good, talking sheer common sense!

But he had been too stupid to understand!

He suddenly could not bear to remain in the Library which had seemed to him more essentially his father's than any other room in the house, and turning towards the door he had gone upstairs to bed.

He was sleeping, because it was expected of him, in the room that the Masters of Barons' Hall had always used.

Dawkins was waiting up for him, and a fire was burning brightly, piled with logs cut on the Estate.

He remembered as a child how he had watched the woodmen at work, cheering as they felled a tree; getting in the way as they chopped off the branches and cut it into lengths to be carried to the saw-mills.

"A fire, Dawkins?" he asked in surprise.

"The wind blows cold tonight, M'Lord, and these May winds can be treacherous, when you're not used to them."

That, he thought, was the operative phrase – "not used to them" – he who had grown soft with living in the sun.

It was only by concentrating fiercely on taking exercise, riding until his horse and himself were exhausted, and swimming in the sea, that he had kept his muscles in good condition.

Dawkins was right.

He felt the cold more than he would have if he had lived always in England, and despite all his efforts the sun had in some ways undermined his stamina.

He undressed in silence and, as if to defy his Valet, he had gone to the windows to pull back the curtains and open the casement.

The blustery coldness of the wind took him almost by surprise and it made him cough.

"Now, M'Lord, you're taking foolish risks," Dawkins admonished him. "You know what the Doctor said when you were so ill that winter in Naples."

Lord Damien turned from the window.

He had been so ill that winter in Naples, not because of the climate but because he had fought a duel over Phenice and his opponent had been a better shot than he was.

Dawkins left him and he lay on the great four-poster bed in which the Masters of Barons' Hall had slept for over a hundred years.

It had been designed when the house had been re-decorated, and he had always thought that the bed posts, carved and gilded in imitation of palm trees, had been romantic.

That was until he was sick of palm trees – sick of their branches waving against a cloudless sky, sick of their barren trunks up which the natives climbed like monkeys to pluck the coconuts.

He longed for English oak trees which had stood hundreds of years, beeches with their red leaves, limes, elms, ash – anything rather than the trees like palms that belonged to a hot tropical climate.

The fire cast strange patterns on the ceiling and then changed to images.

He could see the first palazzo where they had lived in Venice.

He thought he would never be tired of looking out at the Canal through the ancient windows. It had been so beautiful, so poetical, and he had searched the book-shops to find poems to read to Phenice to which she would not listen.

"Do not waste time on poems, Virgil. Kiss me! Tell me you love me! Make me feel!"

He could hear her voice inflaming him with its passionate undertones and later the same voice repeating over the years.

"Virgil, I am bored! Let us go somewhere else!"

"Virgil, let us have a party – it is so boring to be alone!"

"Virgil, make me feel – excite me! It is all I live for!"

That was the truth! He found that all that Phenice lived for was the feelings which not only he, but other men, could arouse in her.

> "In her first passion woman loves her lover;
> In all the others all she loves is love."

The images cast by the flames shifted: he saw the first time he realised she was unfaithful. He had called the man out, shot him down savagely!

Only when he saw the blood oozing in a crimson flood over his white shirt did he ask himself how he could be so uncivilised, or behave so brutally to another human being.

Then there had been Phenice crying, pleading, begging his forgiveness.

"I did not mean to do it – it just – happened! Oh! Virgil, it is your – fault. You do not make me – love you, you do not excite me as you used to do!"

It was a cry that was to be repeated and repeated. There were always other men, other infidelities, other suspicions that gnawed in his mind like some terrible canker.

Then, worse, came the conviction that what he suspected was true; and finally and most degrading of all, a wanting not to know, not to be sure, to ignore what was occurring.

They were together for six years in which, Virgil thought later, he grew from an ignorant, idealistic, foolish boy into a cynical, bitter old man!

He thought after six years with Phenice there was nothing he did not know about women. Nothing she had not taught him; nothing that she had not soiled, cheapened and degraded.

When she left him he had hated himself because he would not face the truth that he was glad.

She had not run away, she had merely told him indifferently she was going with a man he had suspected of being her lover for some months.

He was an Egyptian, immensely rich, passionate, demanding and undoubtedly brutal. That was what Phenice craved. Brutality! While he had offered her gentleness.

Once he had hit her when she had driven him almost crazy with her provocative behaviour with another man.

Immediately he had been appalled that he should have done such a thing. It was against every instinct not only of his mind but of his breeding.

It was only as he dropped on his knees beside the couch on which she lay with a vivid crimson mark on her face where he had struck her, apologising, begging her forgiveness, that he had realised almost in horror, she had enjoyed it!

She had wanted to be conquered, for him to be far more demanding than he could ever be because it was against his character.

He could be masterful, he could be dominating in love, but that was a very different thing from treating a woman as if she was a chattel and of no account except as a play-thing.

Yet Phenice wanted a man who was heartless, a cruel tyrant to whom she could surrender herself as if she was his captive slave.

Virgil had found her supervising the packing while her two maid-servants filled her trunks. He had ordered them from the room and then looked at Phenice for an explanation.

"There is no reason to send them away, they know I am going with Salin."

"Do you think you will be happy with him?"

She shrugged her shoulders.

"As happy as I can be with anyone. He is immensely rich, I shall never want for anything while I am with him."

"I have given you everything you wanted."

Virgil had a large fortune of his own, left him by his mother, and there was no question of his father cutting him off with the proverbial shilling.

"Money and jewels are not really what I want," Phenice said and a smile curved her lips.

"I know what you want," Virgil said harshly, "and I am quite ready to admit that I am not the sort of man to give it to you!"

"You are too English to understand!" she answered. "If I do not go now I shall be too old! Too old to make a change!"

For once she was speaking truthfully.

One of the things he had learnt in those six years they had been together was that she had lied about her age as she had lied about so many things.

She had told him that she was twenty-six, admitting it shyly as a young girl might have done.

But he did not need to be a mathematician to realise, as she talked of what she had done and places she had been, that she was at least six years older.

Now she was thirty-eight and he knew that the thought of old age was as terrifying as if every time she looked in the glass she was confronting a skull.

She watched her face for every wrinkle, searched her head in case one hair had turned grey.

She used every artifice, every cosmetic that was sold, and this last year she had haunted quacks who offered the Elixir of Youth at ten guineas a box.

That was the dragon that Phenice wanted him to kill for her but even his ardour and his love had not been enough to arrest the hand of time.

The Egyptian was not more than twenty-five. He would learn, Virgil had thought dryly, as he had learnt.

The one thing Phenice craved from him was his passion and fire of youth which would give her the illusion that once again she was young.

When she had finally gone and there was only the seductive scent she had always used lingering on the atmosphere, Virgil had felt not only relieved, but also a loneliness that he had not anticipated.

The palazzo, not the same one they had rented six years earlier, but another more elaborate and more expensive, had seemed very quiet – frighteningly quiet.

He always expected to hear her voice calling him.

"Virgil – I am bored!"

"Virgil – ask people to dine with us, dozens and dozens of people!"

"I want a party, I want music, laughter and noise!"

And then inevitably:

"Virgil, make love to me. Make me feel! Set me on fire! I am afraid! Afraid I cannot feel any more!"

He had now given parties on his own, noisy drunken parties which he thought would dispel the loneliness, but instead made it worse.

Then he began to find it impossible to escape from his memories of Barons' Hall.

Instead of the shrill and drunken laughter of his so-called friends, he could hear wood-pigeons cooing to each other in the trees: the rooks coming to roost at sun-set: see the deer scampering across the Park, and hear the horses neighing in the Stables!

He had written to his father twice since he left home, but neither letter had been answered.

But from England friends whom he met in Rome and Paris told him the scandal he had caused and the dignified behaviour of the Marquess who never mentioned his name.

He left Venice finding it intolerable and set off to explore the world. It was something he had always wanted to do and now he was his own master without any encumbrance.

He would seek what he had lost. He did not find it, but he gained experience.

He suffered a great deal of acute discomfort, to find his soul elevated by the beauty of the East, while his mind was often sickened by the poverty, the ignorance and the cruelty.

He travelled in leaking ships; he crossed mountains which hitherto had been impassable with yaks which had to be dragged along razor-edge tracks by porters who grumbled every inch of the way.

It was often very dangerous, but he felt that in some ways he was testing himself, sweeping away the years of indolence and soft living.

Then invariably there were women and he was back in the old haunts because of them.

Venice, Rome, Naples, Paris! Women, always women! Women who gave him illusion of the love that he had once known and which Phenice had killed.

Killed slowly, tortuously, so that it died leaving scars on his mind, on his heart and his soul which would never heal.

But they taught him the same lesson, that beauty is only an illusion and that desire dies as quickly as it is aroused.

Women, more women, filling part of his life and emptying his pocket, but none of them, when he thought back, really touching any vital part of him as Phenice had done.

Sometimes he almost regretted that he was no longer subject to her magic, to her strange allure that could send a man mad with desire.

Then, when he learnt that she was dead, it meant nothing! *"I am ashes where once I was fire."*

It was hard to believe that when he was told that she had killed herself, it meant no more than to hear of the death of an acquaintance he could barely remember.

"What happened?" he had asked, and was surprised his voice sounded so indifferent, so unmoved.

"Salin left her. Then there were other men, but they

became harder and harder to get. The life she had always led caught up with her. She began to drink and took drugs to stimulate herself to wilder excesses."

Virgil could see it all clearly and it seemed incredible that by now Phenice would have been forty-five! Forty-five!

It was then that he knew he would go home.

It had seemed impossible, even after he had learnt on his return from India that his father was dead.

How could he meet those who would ask why he had come alone, or face the Marquess still alive, still married to the woman who had left him for the boy who lived next door!

It was only when he had walked into Barons' Hall that he realised just as nothing was changed in the house, nothing was changed outside.

Phenice might be dead, but the doors of his neighbours would be closed against him because of what happened twelve years earlier.

He would not have known this so positively if he had not stopped in London on his way to the country.

"Good heavens! Virgil, is it you?" a man who had been at Eton with him exclaimed, when he had walked into his Club.

"Anstruther! How are you?" he had replied.

"I should be asking you that question," Roger Anstruther replied, "but there is no need for you to tell me. You look just as you always did, if rather better-looking!"

Virgil had laughed.

"I suppose I should be flattered that you actually remember me."

"We have certainly not been allowed to forget you!"

"What do you mean by that?"

"You have become almost a legend!"

Virgil had been ingenuous enough to ask for an explanation, and he had in fact been quite astounded at what his friend told him.

He had no idea that his parties, or what were called 'orgies' – the women who had followed Phenice – the duels – the scandals – had all percolated from the Continent back to London.

Roger Anstruther had been brutally frank.

"Your old friends, like myself, will be delighted to see you, Virgil. But the women will not accept you!"

Lord Damien had raised his eye-brows.

"The women?" he questioned.

"Well, my wife for instance. I might insist that you dine alone with us, but she could not ask you to meet her women friends. You are taboo, old boy! After all, you did run off with the Lord Lieutenant's wife!"

"A long time ago," Virgil remarked.

"Not too long for the memories of the older hostesses. Besides the Marquess has become more important than ever. He is the Leader of the Government in the House of Lords, and I am sure that while he is alive you do not have a chance of being reinstated!"

Lord Damien was well aware of what social ostracism meant. He had already encountered it in Italy where the best families would not receive Phenice or him.

In Paris and in Venice only the hangers-on, those who would go to any party whoever gave it and the men and women who belonged to the cosmopolitan half-world, accepted their invitations.

Once he knew what to expect, Lord Damien had left London.

As he drove past the great iron gates surmounted with the Lynmouth Crest he had thought that the Marquess had his revenge in a more subtle and certainly more effective manner than if he had challenged him to a duel!

On entering Barons' Hall he walked back into the past, but he had known that the past as far as he was concerned was still the present and likely to be the future.

Phenice was dead but it seemed she still held him prisoner, he would never be free of her.

This was his punishment! This was the retribution he had to pay for the wrong he had done!

As he lay in his father's bed the first night he slept at Barons' Hall he thought the sooner he died the better!

In the morning he tried to sweep such thoughts from him, knowing that they were unhealthy and rather over-dramatic.

But as he went round the great house which was unchanged since he was a child, he knew he had betrayed it as he had betrayed his father.

He did not attempt to excuse himself or put the blame on Phenice.

He only realised cynically that at nineteen he would have been superhuman to withstand her desire for him.

At the same time everything for which he had been educated should have given him enough self-control to know that while she took possession of his body, some part of him still belonged to Barons' Hall and his ancestry.

He looked at his father's portrait.

It was a remarkable likeness and he thought that he appeared rather severe and disapproving as he must have looked whenever he thought of his only son.

"Forgive me!" Virgil said in his heart.

Tired of walking round the garden, he had the following day ordered a horse and ridden over the Park and to some isolated parts of the Estate.

He could not bring himself to call on the Farmers, feeling sure that he would see the condemnation in their faces because he had not been home for so many years.

They would know the reason why! They would talk about him, point a finger of scorn, and he knew he could not face them.

He had ridden all day, and in consequence slept better than he had the first night. For the first time there was a touch of peace percolating the torment which seemed to make his whole body and mind a battle-field.

He must try to decide what he should do.

Should he go, or should he stay?

Should he fill the house with people who would accept him and ignore those who would not?

There would be a Society of sorts, as there had been in Rome and Naples, who would welcome any man with money, especially a Nobleman.

It would not matter how decadent or debauched he was! There would always be companions to keep pace with him.

Perhaps that was the only thing that was left. More parties, more women.

Women! Women! Women! All alike!

He knew before he spoke to them it would be impossible to find in any what he sought.

Then unexpectedly, amazingly, like a drop of dew on the petal of a flower, he had found Gracila!

Chapter Five

Gracila woke up laughing and realised she had been dreaming.

It was all a mix-up of what had happened yesterday which made her laugh until the tears ran down her cheeks.

She and Lord Damien had been down at the stream and he had been fishing for trout.

He had, the previous day, found his old trout-rods in the Gun-room and carried them late at night down through the gardens to the stream and hidden them in the long grass.

In the morning he had ordered Sampson as usual to go riding, telling Millet that he would be out for luncheon but would like to take some sandwiches with him.

As if Millet had been aware that he did not wish to be seen too often, if at all, in the local Inns, he had hurried away to instruct Mrs. Bates, the old cook who had been at the Hall for nearly fifty years, to prepare a luncheon his Lordship could carry in his saddle-bag.

A few minutes later the news reached Gracila that His Lordship would be out until late in the afternoon and she could therefore go into the garden.

"It is such a lovely day," she had said to Mrs. Hansell, "I wonder if I can take something with me to eat? It is a bother to have to come home when I am enjoying the sunshine."

"I'm sure Mrs. Bates will cook something to please you, M'Lady," Mrs. Hansell answered, "and I've a small picnic-basket which will be just what you want to carry."

It was with a feeling of almost irrepressible excitement that an hour later, as soon as she learnt that Lord Damien had left the house, Gracila had crossed the lawn holding the small picnic-basket in her hand.

"Don't go too far, M'Lady," Mrs. Hansell admonished before she left her Bedroom. "It'll be hot in the middle of the day. I thinks we're in for a heat-wave after the cold two nights ago. It may mean a thunder-storm."

"If there is one, I will shelter somewhere," Gracila promised, "so do not worry if I do not come back to the house."

She thought as she walked among the shrubs that she had provided for every emergency. Then she quickened her pace because she was so anxious to see Lord Damien again.

In fact she felt as if there were wings on her heels and she wanted to dance from sheer happiness.

Every day it had been more exciting, more thrilling, to be with him and at night she had dreamt of him as she had last night – a dream which had made her laugh.

What had happened the morning before was that a fish had taken his fly and he had started to play it, forgetting the over-hung branches of the trees.

The point of the rod had been caught in them and as he staggered about, determined not to lose the trout and getting his line more and more entangled, Gracila had found it funny.

She had laughed and laughed and he had laughed too, but finally the trout had got away taking with it the fly fast stuck in its mouth.

"How dare you laugh at me!" Lord Damien had asked when he got his breath.

"You have no idea how funny you looked," Gracila answered.

Then they were both laughing, finding it irresistibly humorous simply because they were sharing the joke.

The whole thing had been enchanting, Gracila thought now.

Lord Damien had caught two more trout which they had cooked in dock-leaves over a fire and it seemed very funny when they both burnt their fingers and while one trout was over-cooked the other was burnt.

There was plenty to eat with the sandwiches which had been provided for His Lordship and the pies and a little bowl of jelly which Mrs. Bates had provided for her.

They had shared everything including a bottle of wine.

Lord Damien had even insisted she had a tiny drink of brandy from his flask which he told her had been laid down in the cellar in his grandfather's time and was the finest Napoleon brandy obtainable.

She had not really liked it but had sipped it to please him, and then he had raised his flask to say:

"To your laughter and to your eyes! The two most beautiful things in the world!"

She had flushed and found it hard to look at him.

After that there had been a poignant little silence in which there seemed to be nothing to say to each other and Gracila knew that something very strange had happened to her heart.

These little silences happened all the afternoon, and Gracila thought that the sun was more golden and the flowers more brilliant than she had ever remembered them.

Before they returned home, Lord Damien said:

"I was thinking last night of what would happen if it rained and we were unable to leave the house."

"I had thought of that too," Gracila said in a low voice.

"Have you suggestions as to how we could meet?"

She shook her head.

"Mrs. Hansell would think it strange if I went out in the pouring rain, and anyway I am certain the Summer-house leaks."

"Then you must listen to my idea," Lord Damien said.

She thought he was pleased that he could solve the problem which she found impossible.

Gracila raised her eyes to his and listened.

"I cannot think why I have not thought of it before," he said, "except that it has not been necessary."

"Thought of what?"

"That you can reach the West Wing quite easily without anyone seeing you."

"I would have to pass the top of the stairs and there is usually a Footman in the Hall."

He smiled almost triumphantly.

"That is where you are wrong! You do not have to pass the top of the stairs."

"Why not?"

"Because you can go up to the top floor."

Gracila gave a little cry.

"I never thought of that!"

"I explored it last night after dinner," he said. "Although it is somewhat dusty, you can walk straight along the top of the house, past the servants' old rooms and descend the staircase at the end of the West Wing."

"I know exactly where that is!" Gracila exclaimed. "It comes out opposite the Library!"

"Exactly! And that is where we will meet each other."

"In the Library?"

"I shall be waiting for you."

"That will be wonderful! And as it happens I need some more books. I have read all the ones there were in the Elizabethan Room."

"Why did you not tell me?"

Gracila laughed.

"What could you have done about it? Order Millet to bring them upstairs to the lady who is staying with you?"

"I would like to have brought them myself," Lord Damien said in a low voice.

"With Mrs. Hansell sleeping next door? You know what she would say!"

He realised that Gracila was taking what he said as a child might have done.

She was so innocent and so pure it never struck her that he might have very different reasons to wish to come to her Bedroom!

"We will meet in the Library," he said aloud, "but I am rather hurt that the only reason you wish to come there is to find a book! I hoped that I rated a little higher!"

"You do," Gracila replied instantly. "At the same time, the evenings when I am alone would seem very long if I could not read!"

"Instead, thanks to my brilliance, you will now be able to talk to me!"

"That will be more wonderful! I want you to tell me more about the places you have visited, and perhaps we could find books about them in the Library?"

"There is certainly a book on India," he admitted, "which will interest you, and I will search for others."

Gracila clapped her hands together.

"It is the most exciting thing that has ever happened to me. Now I will not have to use my imagination to visualise all the places you talk about, but I can listen to you and look at the same time!"

He wondered how many other women would meet him secretly with no other thought but to learn geography.

It was a new experience and he realised that he longed to tell her not only about India and all the other places in the world he had been, but about love.

It was then he knew that he was not only in love with Gracila but she had evoked in him emotions that he had never felt before for any other woman.

Now he knew that the idealism he had known as a boy was back in his mind and heart but it was deeper, more realistic, more human and yet in its own way divine.

Gracila was like a flower, he told himself, a flower that could so easily be hurt or bruised by rough fingers or tempestuous winds.

It struck him, too, that talking to her was like listening to the opening chords of a melody which lingered in his ears long after he had left her.

Her eyes that were raised to his were honest and clear, they were the eyes of a child; the eyes of truth.

It was her innocence and purity that drew him, but he knew as a man he longed to awaken her to womanhood.

His eyes lingered on her lips and as if she sensed what he was feeling, Gracila looked away from him and the flush rose in her cheeks.

With an effort Lord Damien rose to say abruptly:

"We had better tidy up the remains of our meal, otherwise a casual passer-by might suspect that a feast had taken place!"

"The most delicious feast I have ever eaten."

"That is what I found," he replied, "and very satisfying!"

He thought of the money he had expended on the huge parties he had given in Venice and on what had been termed as 'orgies' in Paris, with the champagne flowing and delicacies collected from every part of the world to tempt the jaded appetites of the diners.

There had been the inevitable headache in the morning, not only from the wine but from the smoke of cigars and the indulgences of the flesh!

Pictures flashed through his mind which made him recoil almost in horror in case Gracila should be aware of what he was thinking.

Then he told himself that he had only to raise his eyes from the dirt, squalor and debauchery to the stars, and especially to one particular little star who was different from all the rest.

To Gracila his changes of mood, his silences and the look in his eyes were all part of an enchantment which held her spell-bound.

Never had she realised before that a man could be so handsome, so masculine, but at the same time enter into that part of her mind she had kept secret because no one else had ever understood.

Lord Damien had not only listened, but had made many things clearer to her.

So inevitably when the time came when they must leave each other, she had gone back to the house feeling as if her mind had expanded and he had lifted her high into the sky in a way no-one had ever done before.

'I shall see him very shortly,' Gracila thought as Mrs. Hansell came into the room to draw back the curtains.

"A wet day, M'Lady," she said. "I was expecting it after the thunder-storm last night!"

"Was there a thunder-storm?" Gracila asked.

"There was indeed, M'Lady, and torrential rain followed it. The gardens are all awash."

Gracila smiled, knowing that yesterday she would have been dismayed at the thought she could not go out. But now they could meet, as Lord Damien had suggested, in the Library!

"There's terrible news, M'Lady!" Mrs. Hansell went on, pulling back the second curtain.

"What has happened?"

Gracila had a sudden fear that her hiding-place had been discovered.

"It's the Queen, M'Lady. We might have lost her."

"The Queen?" Gracila repeated, not understanding.

"The newspapers have just come and have reported that a madman fired at Her Majesty in the Park."

"Did he hurt her?" Gracila gasped.

Mrs. Hansell shook her head.

"God was merciful, but the Queen was that brave one could hardly credit the danger to which she submitted herself."

"Tell me," Gracila asked with interest. "Tell me exactly what happened."

She had been interested in the young Queen ever since she had come to the throne.

Six years earlier it had been fascinating to learn how restricted and cloistered Princess Victoria had been by her mother until, when the King had died and she was only eighteen, she had moved overnight from the School-room to the throne!

Gracila was no exception as the whole country had thought that young Victoria was like a Fairy-Queen, and that in her reign a new era would bring peace and prosperity to England.

From Castle to cottage stories of the Queen were repeated and re-repeated; sketches of her in the newspapers or oleographs which were sold in the shops were treasured and to be found everywhere.

There was the Coronation to thrill everyone and then, even more exciting, the wedding to the man she loved.

There was not a girl in England who did not feel that the Queen, in marrying Albert, had opened the gate-way to love, rather than being forced into an arranged marriage as happened not only with Royalty but in every aristocratic family in the land.

Gracila had asked herself now why she had not been more insistent on choosing her own husband, as the Queen had done, rather than accept the Duke just because her father and Step-mother had thought him the right sort of husband for her.

Yet now the young Queen, carrying the enormous burden of monarchy on her slim shoulders, had been in danger!

"What has happened?" Gracila asked before Mrs. Hansell could speak.

"Apparently," Mrs. Hansell began, delighted to be an informant, "from what Millet has read me, Her Majesty saw, the day before yesterday while she and Prince Albert were adriving in the Mall, a swarthy, ill-looking rascal pointing a pistol at her."

"Did he fire it?" Gracila asked.

"No," Mrs. Hansell replied. "Apparently it misfired and the man slipped away in the crowd."

"Surely someone could have detained him?" Gracila asked indignantly.

"One would have thought so, M'Lady," Mrs. Hansell replied. "If you ask me, they're far too casual with Her Majesty's safety."

"Please go on, Mrs. Hansell."

"Well, according to the newspapers, Her Majesty felt certain he'd try again, and, though the Prince tried to dissuade her, she couldn't endure being shut up with this danger hanging over her head."

"I can understand that," Gracila murmured.

"So yesterday," Mrs. Hansell continued, "the Royal couple drove out exactly as they'd done before, except that the Queen left her Lady-in-Waiting, Lady Portman, behind."

"That was thoughtful of her."

"I always knew in my bones Her Majesty'd be very considerate," Mrs. Hansell said.

"What happened?"

"The man fired again, but this time at five paces."

"And he did not hit her?"

"No! the gun only made a slight click and then he was seized. The Press think that it was in fact unloaded."

"Unloaded!" Gracila exclaimed. "Then he must have been mad!"

"That's what the reports say, but we'll know more when he comes up for trial."

"It is frightening to think what might have happened," Gracila said in a low voice.

"There should be Services of Thanksgiving in every Church in the land," Mrs. Hansell declared.

"I agree with you," Gracila said. "We could not bear to lose the Queen."

There was something romantic and exciting in having a young woman on the throne after the aged and red-faced William IV who did not really look like a King at all.

"I am glad, so very glad the Queen is safe!" Gracila said with feeling.

"Yes, it'd have been a real tragedy if Her Majesty couldn't have come here tomorrow."

"Tomorrow!" Gracila exclaimed.

"You must have known, M'Lady, that she's opening the Hospital in Newbury and then attending a Garden Party given by the Lord Lieutenant, the Marquess of Lynmouth."

"Oh! Of course!" Gracila said. "I heard it talked about, but I had forgotten the date."

And then it suddenly struck her that today, the 31st of May, was to have been her wedding day!

It was not surprising she had forgotten, in the excitement of her own ceremony, that the Queen was coming to the County, because she had thought that she would not be there but already on her honeymoon.

Now she recalled her Step-mother talking about it and saying it was a good thing they had not chosen June 1st for the wedding as it would have had to be postponed, and that would have undoubtedly been unlucky.

So to-day she was to have married the Duke and the unlucky postponement had in fact happened, though in Gracila's mind it was extremely lucky.

At this very moment she might have been dressing for a marriage with a man who was only interested in her Step-mother.

She felt herself shiver.

She had not realised then what marriage could mean. But now she knew with complete certainty that marriage must be based on love.

Mrs. Hansell brought in her breakfast tray and set it down by the side of her bed.

"I've been thinking so much of Her Majesty, M'Lady," she said in an apologetic tone, "that I was forgetting that this should have been your wedding-day!"

"Think how dismal it would have been," Gracila answered, looking towards the window. "I would not have been able to drive through the Village in an open carriage and that would have spoilt a lot of people's fun."

"You don't regret running away, M'Lady?"

"No! Of course not!" Gracila replied. "I am so grateful that I found out in time that I could not marry the Duke, and you and Mitty were kind enough to take care of me."

"But you'll have to have a husband some time, M'Lady," Mrs. Hansell said. "I was only saying to Millet last night that I've never seen you look so lovely. It must be the rest and all the fresh air you're having."

"It is because I am so happy here," Gracila said and added as an after-thought, "with you both!"

She knew she was not quite telling the truth.

There was someone else who had made her happy; someone she was aching to be with, with an intensity that seemed to grow every minute that passed.

"As it's raining, M'Lady," Mrs. Hansell was saying, "I was thinking it would be a good thing this morning if we worked in the Still-room, and you could help me, as you promised, with making some of the preserves."

It was in fact something that Gracila had suggested the first day after she had come to Barons' Hall.

She had thought it would please Mrs. Hansell and also occupy the long hours when she would be forced to sit in the house because they were not certain where His Lordship would be.

Mrs. Hansell had been too busy at the time, and now Gracila knew it would be difficult to find an excuse for not doing what she wished.

Because the House-keeper was waiting for her reply she said after a moment:

"It will be fun to work in the Still-room this morning, and this afternoon, if it is still raining, I can have a rest."

"Now that's really sensible, M'Lady!" Mrs. Hansell answered, "and I'll be busy this afternoon as it happens, as I've told Hetty that we have to turn out the linen cupboard. It'd slipped my attention, what with His Lordship arriving home unexpected-like and Your Ladyship coming to stay."

"I am afraid I have been a great trouble for you," Gracila smiled, knowing that Mrs. Hansell would deny such an accusation.

It was infuriating to be working in the Still-room when she might have been with Lord Damien, but she had a feeling he would not expect her and later she heard that despite the rain he had at 11 o'clock gone out for an hour's ride.

That, she told herself, was when he had given up expecting her in the morning. But she felt sure that he would wait for a long time in the afternoon.

She was so excited by the thought of seeing him that it was difficult to eat the delicious dishes Mrs. Bates had prepared for her luncheon.

It seemed so ridiculous that she was sitting alone in her little Sitting-room while Lord Damien was downstairs alone in the Dining-room.

It would be so wonderful to be together, Gracila thought, laughing and talking.

There were a thousand things she wanted to say to him and for which there was never time.

Mrs. Hansell collected her tray.

"Now you have a nice rest, M'Lady, as you suggested, and don't go wearing your eyes out with one of them books. Sleep is what you need!"

"I will try to do what you tell me," Gracila answered.

Mrs. Hansell carried away the tray and Gracila went into her Bedroom next door.

There she stood waiting until she could no longer hear the House-keeper's rather heavy footsteps going down the passage.

Then she turned the key in the lock and put it in her pocket just in case Mrs. Hansell returned.

Then tiptoeing, although she was quite certain there was no-one to hear her, she slipped down the passage to the stairs that led to the second floor and then to the third.

As Lord Damien had told her, the passage which ran

along the top of the house was dusty and the doors of the rooms which had once housed three dozen House-, Kitchen- and Scullery-maids were all closed.

It was rather ghostly and Gracila hurried along the passage which twisted and turned as she moved from one part of the original building to another.

But at last she reached the other end of the great house and found a staircase almost identical to the one she had climbed descending to the second floor, and then again to the first and finally to the ground.

This, Gracila thought, was the only time she was in any danger of being seen. Millet or a Footman might be waiting on His Lordship in the Library.

But when she peeped round the side of the stairway, the wide corridor which led to the Hall was empty and beyond the Library, which was built at the end of the house, was only the Orangery.

She slipped across the corridor and opened the door.

Lord Damien was there waiting for her.

"Gracila! I knew you would come."

He sprang up from the high chair he had been sitting on and she had an instinctive desire to run towards him and into his arms.

With an effort she forced herself to shut the door quietly behind her and then move with decorum to the fireplace.

"I knew you would come," he repeated. "I waited this morning and then went riding."

"Yes, I know. Mrs. Hansell asked me to help her in the Still-room and I did not like to refuse."

They were talking commonplaces but their eyes were saying very different things.

Because she felt shy at the expression in his eyes, Gracila turned round to look at the great room.

"Every time I come here to the Library," she said, "I think how lovely this room is, and ever since I can re- member I have looked up at the goddesses on the ceiling and thought what fun they were having floating on the clouds with all those cupids."

She turned up her face as she spoke and the long line of her neck made Lord Damien draw in his breath.

Then suddenly, inexplicably, in a voice she had never heard from him before, he said:

"For God's sake do not look like that because I cannot bear it!"

"Like what?" Gracila enquired in surprise.

"I have been waiting for you feeling that every moment was like the passing of a century," he said, "and now when I see you here, I know that I have to go away."

"Go away!" Gracila repeated, "but why, I do not understand?"

"Because I cannot meet you like this! Because it is wrong for you – and hell for me!"

Gracila looked at him in consternation.

"I still do not ... understand."

"Then let me put it more plainly," he said and his voice was raw. "I love you, Gracila! I love you in a manner I have never loved before and never will again! But I have nothing to offer you."

For a moment she thought she could not have heard him aright and then Gracila's face became radiant as if a thousand candles lit her eyes.

"You ... love ... me?" she whispered.

"Do you expect me to do anything else?" he enquired. "Oh! my darling, I did not know it was possible there was anyone like you in the whole world, so pure, so perfect, so innocent! And that is why you are not for me!"

"You ... love me," Gracila said, "and I know ... now that ... I ..."

Her voice died away and he said:

"Say it! Say it and let me hear it just once so that I can remember it for the rest of my life!"

"I ... love ... you," she said, "but I did not ... really know it was ... love and yet I suppose I did."

He stood looking at her and she thought it was impossible that a man's eyes could hold such pain in their depths.

"You do ... love ... me?" she asked, almost like a child who is afraid she has misheard what she had been told.

"I love you so that my whole body is a battle-ground and I am torn in pieces!" Lord Damien replied.

"Th . then ... then ... why must ... you ... go ... away?"

"I have told you I have nothing to offer you."

She stood looking at him, her eyes shining, and he stared at her for a long moment before he said:

"I know what you are thinking, but, my precious, perfect love, it is impossible! How could I offer you marriage and what sort of marriage would it be for you?"

"I love you," Gracila answered, "and I now know why I could never ... marry anyone but ... you."

"That is not true," he said sharply. "You will marry, of course you will marry, a man who is worthy of your beauty."

"Never, if I did not love him!" she replied.

"You are so young," he said, "you do not understand love as I understand it, and you will forget me!"

"Never! Never!" Gracila interrupted. "You are the man I have always longed for and believed existed somewhere in the world. You are the man I have seen when I have read books, but only in my mind. But now my dreams are ... real and you are ... here!"

"Stop!" Lord Damien commanded, "Stop saying such things to me. You are tempting me, Gracila, to forget that I have some decency left, though the Lord knows it is not much!"

"You have suffered," Gracila said, "but perhaps ... I can make ... you happy."

Lord Damien put his hand up to his face as if he would shut out the pleading look in her eyes and the movement of her lips. Then he said:

"Try to be sensible, Gracila. Think what life with me would be like. Ostracised by every decent person, wandering from place to place and never having a real home! Never belonging!"

"We can live here," she said softly.

"And every door in the County shut against us? With people pointing a finger of scorn whenever you went through the gates into the world outside?"

He looked at her and said:

"Do you think my love is so feeble that I would sacrifice you rather than myself? My darling, I have said I love you and that means I will go away. I will leave tomorrow! Or if I had any sense, tonight!"

"No!" Gracila cried, "I cannot ... bear it! I cannot ... lose you!"

She saw by the expression on his face that he was determined to do what he said, and frantically, because she felt her happiness was slipping from her, she went on:

"I have never told you why I am here, and you have never asked me."

"I wanted you to trust me," he said simply.

"I have trusted you and I do trust you, but I want to trust you ... with my ... whole life."

"Tell me what you are going to tell me," he said as if he could not bear to answer what she had just said.

"I am Gracila Shering," she replied, "my father, the Earl of Sheringham, was a great friend of your father."

"I remember him," Lord Damien said briefly.

"My mother died, and my father married for the third time someone I never liked," Gracila continued.

She found it difficult to tell her story, feeling that whatever she said would make no difference to Lord Damien's decision and that he was not really interested in anything except the suffering of parting from her.

Quickly, stumbling a little, she told him how she had accepted the decision that she should marry the Duke.

How only when she had overheard the Duke and her

Step-mother in the Library at the Castle, did she know that marriage in such circumstances was impossible.

"I had nowhere to go," Gracila finished, "nowhere until I thought of Millet who had been with us ever since I can remember."

"So he hid you here, in Barons' Hall," Lord Damien said.

"At first he refused," Gracila answered, "until I told him that I was afraid to go to London ... alone with no ... money."

"How could you run away under such circumstances?"

"What ... else could I do?"

"You are right, of course you are right," he said. "But to come here, and find that I was here too, was somehow unfortunate!"

Gracila drew in her breath.

"I think it was fate," she said, "fate that we should meet and find we ... belong ... to each ... other."

The colour rose in her cheeks as she said the last words.

"Perhaps in some previous life that might have been true," Lord Damien answered, "but not now, not at this moment!"

He threw out his hands as if in defiance of what had happened before and said:

"God knows it is a punishment I deserve! Punishment that exactly fits the crime! I have found you, now I have to leave you!"

"How can you do ... this to ... us?" Gracila asked. "How can you ... go away and leave ... me?"

"Because I cannot stay and love you."

He made a sound that was half a cry, half a groan.

"It has been hard enough to be with you as long as I have and not touch you, not kiss you."

"Why do you ... not do ... so?"

"Because I love you enough not to want to make you unhappy."

"By ... leaving me?"

"I thought we could go on playing our games together, pretending we were friends and it was fun. But this morning, when you did not come, I knew that it was just a hollow pretence and I was aching, yearning, desperate to see you."

He drew in his breath.

"It was with the utmost difficulty I did not run to your room just to be sure you were there. Just to see your face."

"And I ... wanted you," Gracila said. "I was thinking of you all the time I was making chutney, preserving beetroot and bottling onions."

Lord Damien gave a little choke of laughter as if he could not help himself.

"Oh! my precious!" he exclaimed, "how can you say anything so ridiculously absurd. I want to talk of killing myself and you tell me you were preserving onions!"

"That is life!" Gracila said, "and it is all muddled up together! But just to be with you is so ... wonderful, it is like ... being in Heaven!"

Lord Damien took a step towards her and she thought for a moment he would take her in his arms. But as if his will asserted itself, he asked almost angrily:

"And how long do you think that Heaven would last! You do not understand, but I have endured for twelve years the sort of life we would be forced to live and I can tell you it is not Heaven but Hell!"

Gracila did not speak and he went on:

"Do you imagine I could let you become besmirched by the only type of people who would desire our company? Do you think I could watch you becoming as disillusioned as I have been with life and with love. Love which at the moment seems sacred!"

"It is sacred," Gracila said, "and because I believe it is the love that you have sought, and I have always wanted, it would not be ... lost."

"That is what I know would be impossible," Lord

Damien said, "and because I love you and because, my darling, you are sacred to me, I have got to think sensibly and wisely for us both."

"But why should you go away?"

"Because I cannot stay in England and not see you! And because I cannot be near you for long without breaking down, with all my fine principles and noble ideas scattered to the winds! I am not strong where you are concerned, Gracila, I am weak!"

He sighed before he continued:

"I am a man who is abjectly, hopelessly, crazily in love, and as such not entirely responsible for his actions!"

The passion in his voice made Gracila quiver and now because she could not bear him to suffer, she moved towards him.

"Stay with me ... please ... stay with ... me," she pleaded, turning her face up to his. "I will ... go with you ... anywhere you ... want in the world. I am not afraid of ... anything so long as I can be ... with you."

He looked at her and his face was grim, as if to fight against her offer was almost intolerable.

Then with a wild gesture and a choke as if his voice was strangled in his throat he turned away from her and went towards the window.

"Stop tempting me," he said angrily. "Leave me alone, Gracila, and one day you will remember that it was not the devil that tempted you but you who tempted the devil!"

She knew she had failed.

She stood still where he had left her, feeling as if she was alone in a darkness where there was no light.

"If you are wondering what will happen to me," Lord Damien said, almost as if he was speaking to himself, "you can think of me drinking myself insensible at riotous parties, where I will entertain the hoi polloi, the free drinkers, the hangers-on of Society!"

He spoke bitterly and he continued:

"And there will be women! Of course there will be

women! And perhaps, if I am fortunate, like the wine I drink, they will help me to forget!"

He turned round as he spoke and looked at her. The lines on his face were sharply edged, his mouth contorted by the sneering way in which he had spoken.

Then he saw the expression on Gracila's face and the look in her eyes, as if unexpectedly her whole world had crashed around her and she was alone and afraid.

For a moment he stared at her across the room and then in two strides he was at her side.

"My darling, my precious! Do not look like that," he said, "I did not mean it. I had forgotten to whom I was speaking! I had forgotten that you had no idea of the depths to which a man can sink when he is in despair!"

He put his arms round her as he spoke and with a little murmur, as if she was frightened, Gracila clung to him, her face hidden against his shoulder.

"I love you! I love you so completely, so absolutely," Lord Damien said with his lips on her hair, "that the idea of life without you is a pit of destruction in which I can only hope that I perish quickly."

Gracila made no sound but he knew she was crying.

"Forgive me, my darling! Oh! My darling, forgive me! I am not worth one tear, and that you should cry for me is in a way the most perfect thing that has ever happened."

That his arms were round her and she was close against him seemed to Gracila to be the most wonderful thing that had ever happened.

His words could hardly penetrate the fog that seemed to encompass her mind, but his arms gave her security and a feeling of safety which a moment ago had vanished and left behind a despair that was beyond words.

"How could I hurt you?" Lord Damien asked. "How could I have been so cruel? My little star. I would give my life to save you one moment's unhappiness and yet I have made you cry."

The tenderness in his voice made her tears come faster

and then he put his fingers under her chin and turned her face up to his.

"Look at me, Gracila," he commanded. "Look at me!"

She opened her eyes which were misty with tears which were also on the ends of her curved-back lashes and still ran down her cheeks.

It seemed for a moment as if words had left him and he could not speak.

Then as they looked at each other, their faces very near together, he said gently:

"I love you, and I worship you. You are everything that a man could desire, my little love, my star. You have to believe me when I tell you I cannot spoil anything so beautiful and so holy."

"I love . . . you," Gracila whispered.

"And you said also that you trusted me," Lord Damien said, "and that is why, my lovely one, you have got to trust me to know what is right for you."

"You will go . . . away?"

"I have to," he said, and now his voice was quiet and infinitely sad.

"But how can I live . . . without you? How can I ever be . . . happy if . . . you leave . . . me?"

"You are very young," he said, "and the young forget!"

"Have you . . . forgotten?"

There was a faint smile on his lips as he said:

"You are not only beautiful, my precious one, you are clever, and that is another reason why I love you. No, I have not been able to forget. But I believe that you will be able to do so, and I am doing what is right and what your mother, if she were alive, would want me to do."

"Mama would . . . want me to be . . . happy."

"She would not wish you to take the downward path, which is what you would do if you married me."

Her eyes were on his. Although he still held her close she felt he was moving away from her.

"Please ... please ... marry me," she pleaded.

He pulled her closer and his arms tightened and she thought he was going to kiss her.

Instead he only laid his cheek against her forehead and said in a voice so fraught with suffering that she could hardly recognise it :

"It has to be good-bye my love, my only love, now and for eternity !"

Chapter Six

Gracila stood in her Sitting-room waiting.

Every second or so she looked at the clock on the mantelpiece, knowing that at ten minutes to eleven o'clock she would be able to go down into the garden.

Last night when Lord Damien had told her they had to part, she had heard the misery and despair in his voice and she thought that in that moment she grew up.

She ceased thinking of herself and her own unhappiness but of his.

She knew that once he left her the disillusionment would be back on his face and he had spoken the truth when he said he would go down in a pit of destruction.

Everything that was maternal and compassionate in her told her that she must help him, and yet, distraught by her own unhappiness, it was hard to know what to do.

She longed to stay in his arms knowing that they gave her a feeling of safety that she would never find again.

Then with what was a superhuman effort she fought back the tears and found the strength to say in a very low voice:

"If you must ... leave me will you ... give me a ... present before ... you go?"

"You know I will give you anything it is within my power to give," he answered.

Again the agony that she could not only sense in his words but which emanated from his whole body made her voice a little stronger as she said:

"What I ... want you to give me is ... five hours."

"Five hours?" he questioned in surprise.

She moved, and it was the hardest thing she had ever done, from the shelter of his arms to stand looking at him.

"Tomorrow the Queen comes to Newbury," she explained, "and the staff are going to ask you if they can all go in the Landau first to see Her Majesty when she enters the Hospital, then to stand outside the gates of Lynmouth House."

Lord Damien was listening, but she felt that one part of him was aching for her, yearning for her, because he was no longer touching her.

The pain in his eyes made her long to put her arms around him and hold him close rather than to go on talking.

"They can go – of course they can," he said as if it was too unimportant to consider.

"Then we will be ... alone together," Gracila went on.

She clasped her hands together as if to steady herself as she continued:

"When we part I do not want you to remember our unhappiness, but the times we have laughed by the stream, the times when we argued with each other, capped each other's quotations, and the world seemed ... full of ... sunshine."

She could not prevent a little throb in her voice as she said the last words.

That was what they had found until now – sunshine and laughter.

"That is how I shall always think of you," he said. "The sun on your hair and in your eyes, and your laughter which is the loveliest sound I have ever heard."

"Then will you give me five more hours?" Gracila pleaded. "Five hours to remember that you are not only in my ... heart, but in my ... imagination and for ... ever in my ... mind."

Their eyes met and it was impossible for either of them to think until once again, because she knew what a strain he was putting on himself, Gracila broke the spell to say very softly:

"We must not spoil our memories ... we must not spoil what will always be for me the most perfect ... experience I shall ... ever know."

"You shall have your five hours, my darling," Lord Damien said.

"We will catch and cook trout for our luncheon," Gracila told him, "and when we have done that perhaps we will peep over the boundary-fence and catch a glimpse of the Queen on the lawns of Lynmouth House ... unless of course, the bushes have grown too high."

"You shall see the Queen," Lord Damien promised.

He said it in a way which made Gracila look at him enquiringly.

"There will be no need for you to look over the boundary-fence," he explained, "but you shall have a 'bird's-eye view' of Her Majesty from the Crows' Nest."

"The Crows' Nest?"

"You have told me so much about my own property," Lord Damien said, "that it is gratifying to find one secret of which you are unaware."

"The Crows' Nest sounds ... exciting."

"I believe you will find it so."

"But where is it, and why have I never heard of it before?"

"I dare say my father had forgotten about it," Lord Damien said, "and I am certain I was the last person to use it."

He moved for the first time since he had held her in his arms to stand with his back to the fire which had been lit in the great marble fireplace because the room was cold from the rain and wind outside.

"My grandfather and the second Marquess of Lynmouth," he began, "fell out over the boundary of this large estate which by extraordinary plan in one place encroaches into the Marquess's garden. This was due to the stream which, as you know, twists through the wood then turns almost at right angles towards Lynmouth House."

"Yes, I know that," Gracila said.

"The Marquess wanted to make his boundary on this side of the stream but my grandfather was not unnaturally determined to keep the stream on our estate."

Gracila knew how violently two owners could fight over such an apparently small matter, but of vast importance to them both.

"The two old gentlemen lost their tempers," Lord Damien continued, "and finally the Marquess said: 'I will not have you peeping and peering into my garden, which, I suspect, is the only reason why you are so keen on pushing your boundary almost up to my windows!'"

He smiled before he went on:

"They both became very heated and, I understand, did not speak to each other for the rest of their lives."

"What happened then?" Gracila enquired.

"My grandfather had been in the Navy," Lord Damien replied. "He, therefore, to spite the Marquess, decided to build a 'Crows' Nest' which really would overlook the gardens of Lynmouth House."

"Now I am beginning to understand how I will see the Queen," Gracila smiled.

"The Crows' Nest was erected directly on the boundary in the tallest fir tree that my grandfather could find," Lord Damien said. "I very much doubt if, having proved his point, the old gentleman ever used it himself, but it was a flag of defiance to enrage the Marquess, which it undoubtedly did!"

"And it is still there?"

"It was when I left home," Lord Damien answered, "and in good repair because I had any deficiencies that had been caused by weather or age repaired by the Estate carpenter."

He paused, remembering how useful he had found the

Crows' Nest when he was meeting Phenice secretly and it was difficult, if not impossible, for them to send notes to each other.

They had therefore made an arrangement that when the Marquess had left the house and it was possible for her to come to the boundary fence to meet him, she would put a white handkerchief on the window-sill of her bedroom window."

Her bedroom overlooked the gardens, and waiting in the Crows' Nest Virgil could see the handkerchief and be ready at the boundary fence to take her in his arms.

He had thought so often of those long waits, with his heart beating in anticipation.

The sight of Phenice moving across the lawn with a small sunshade held over her head had made him feel the blood thundering in his temples and a rising excitement that was almost unbearable.

How was he to know that later he would curse the Crows' Nest because its existence had made it so much easier for them to meet?

Now he told himself that to be in the Crows' Nest with Gracila would be to lay yet another ghost, and when in the future he thought of it he would only think of her.

"It sounds very exciting!" Gracila said, almost like a child being promised a special treat. "I have always longed to see the Queen, and as I was to be married I missed attending a Drawing-room at which otherwise I would have been presented last month."

"You will be able to attend one in the future," Lord Damien said.

Again there was the note in his voice which made her want to comfort him.

"That is unlikely," she answered.

"We have not yet decided what you should do when I have left," he said, "but I must persuade you to go home."

"Do not let us talk about it now," she begged, "and I

have no wish to spoil my wonderful present of five hours by discussing anything unpleasant."

"But, darling, I have to think about your future."

Gracila shook her head.

"No!" she said. "You have refused to have any part in it, and therefore you can only concern yourself with the present."

She had sat down as they were talking because she felt as if her legs were too weak to hold her, and now he said:

"You have to be sensible, my lovely one. You cannot go on hiding in Barons' Hall nor, as you mentioned to me once, can you go to London or any other place alone."

"What I need is ... someone to ... look after me," Gracila murmured.

"I know that," he said harshly, "but it cannot be me."

Again she wanted to plead that she might be with him, marry him, to do anything he wished as long as they could be together. But she loved him too much to increase the unhappiness he was feeling and instead she said:

"I want you to think of me as you did at first, as a runaway star, and stars find their own place in the firmament."

She knew that he was about to argue with her, to beg her to be sensible, but instead he bit back the words.

Gracila looked at the clock on the mantelpiece.

"I must go back to my room. Mrs. Hansell will be bringing up my tea in a short while. She would be surprised to find the door locked."

"You will come to me later when they think you have retired?" he asked quickly.

Gracila shook her head.

"It would be better not, we shall only make ourselves ... more unhappy than we are ... already."

She saw the disappointment in his eyes and added:

"We have always been together in the sun. I want to go to sleep looking forward to tomorrow, and thinking of the fun we shall have before we ... have to say ... goodbye."

Lord Damien took a step towards her as if it was such an intolerable idea that once again he must hold her against him. Then she saw his lips tighten and he squared his chin as he said:

"One day when you are older you will understand that my decision is right."

"However old I may grow," Gracila answered, "I shall know that you are a man of high principles; a man who is everything noble and fine, and ... that I love ... honour and ... admire you."

Her voice broke on the last words and she rose and ran from the room before he could prevent her.

Tears blinded her eyes as she ran up the back stairs and along the dusty corridor at the top of the house.

She reached her Bedroom and unlocked the door to throw herself down on her bed to cry until she was exhausted.

It had been an agony late that night not to change her mind and go downstairs.

That he would be alone in the Library and it would be easy to reach him without anyone knowing, was a temptation that she had to resist not only with her will but also with her heart.

Womanlike she knew that her presence would torture him; that to yield to her longing and make him break under the strain would in a way defile his manhood.

She had the feeling that he had never denied his own desires as he was doing at this moment, and that the denial rested on a love that was deeper and greater than anything he had ever felt before.

'We were made for each other,' she thought. 'How can life be so ... cruel as to ... separate us and make us ... live apart?'

Innocent though she was in the ways of the world she knew that the life Lord Damien envisaged they would be forced to live would eventually spoil the perfection of their love.

While love itself might survive, it would not be the Divine, sacred emotion it was at the moment.

It was impossible to sleep, and all through the night Gracila, knowing Lord Damien would be doing the same, found her brain searching every avenue by which they might escape the inevitable and live as they wanted to live – a normal life at Barons' Hall.

Gracila could think of nothing more marvellous than to be with Lord Damien and help him with all the duties and activities which would engage him if he could take his rightful place in the County and in the House of Lords.

Her father was always busy, not only looking after his Estate but attending Committees concerning County affairs of which he was a member, and speaking on subjects on which he was an authority in the House of Lords.

That was the life that would have been Lord Damien's if at nineteen he had not thrown it overboard for a woman who was not worth the sacrifice.

He had never spoken of Phenice directly, but determined to find out a little more about him Gracila had talked with old Mrs. Bates who had been at Barons' Hall long before she was born.

"A lovely young gent'man, he were, M'Lady!" she said when Gracila asked her about Lord Damien as a child, "and when he was growed up it'd be difficult to find a man more handsome in the whole length and breadth of the land!"

She gave a deep sigh as she kneaded her pastry and said:

"We fair doted on him here, and 'twas the shock of our lives when he goes off with Her Ladyship."

"Did you ever see her?" Gracila had asked.

"Aye, I sees her, M'Lady, and the least said about her the better! A woman of her age carryin' on with a boy hardly old enough to shave! Cradle-snatching and a crying shame, as I says the moment I hears of it, and I've not changed me mind now."

Mrs. Bates was full of stories of Christmas parties when 'Master Virgil' would hand out the presents which were given not only to the household staff but to everyone else on the Estate.

She told Gracila of the many kindnesses he had shown to the old people and the trouble he had taken when a boy had been caught poaching to save him from transportation.

"A heart o' gold – that's what Master Virgil had! But of course there was always those as'd take advantage of him," Mrs. Bates finished bitterly.

It was no use trying to step back into the past, Gracila told herself. What she longed for was to be able to help Lord Damien in the future, and yet that was the one thing he denied her.

Half-a-dozen times in the night she rose to look out and see if the rain had stopped, knowing it would spoil everything the next day if the sun was not shining and they were unable to leave the house.

At five o'clock the golden fingers of the dawn in the east began to sweep away the darkness of the night and the stars were fading.

Gracila tried to prevent herself from feeling that it was an omen of hope. What could she hope for except the five hours he had promised to her? Five hours of sunshine!

"We must both enjoy it to the full!" she admonished herself.

She was determined that she would not let him be aware of her despair and the almost frightening intensity of her longing to fight his decision that he must go away.

"How can I let him go? How can I live without him?" she asked.

But she told herself that if she made scenes, if she cried, if she made him more unhappy than he was already it would only hurt him, just as other women had hurt him, especially the Marchioness.

It would have been impossible for her to be alone with Lord Damien these past days without realising that, despite his assertions that he was changed and disillusioned, the spiritual idealism in his nature was still there.

"If we could only be together, it would make him forget the past completely and absolutely," Gracila whispered.

Then she knew that such an idea was as hopeless as her tears had been the night before.

She dressed herself in one of her prettiest gowns, aware that the pale blue of it matched her eyes and accentuated the translucence of her skin.

She arranged her hair very carefully, wanting him to remember it looking like sunshine, and she had already washed away the tell-tale tear-stains from around her eyes.

She knew that she looked her best because she was in love.

She radiated, as he would have said, like a light from a star the feelings within herself.

The hands of the clock on the mantelpiece reached ten minutes to eleven and now she knew she could go.

Lord Damien would already have ridden off on Sampson. The servants would be halfway down the drive in the Landau that was to carry them to Newbury and she was in fact alone in the house.

She picked up the small picnic-basket which Mrs. Hansell had left for her. Then with a last glance at herself in the mirror she ran from her room down the staircase which led to the garden-door.

Everything smelt fresh after the rain of yesterday, the fragrance of lilac scented the air, and the colour of the blossoms not only glowed on the bushes but, scattered by the wind, carpeted the ground.

This morning Gracila did not stop to touch the magnolias or to stare up at the almond trees.

She wanted only to reach Lord Damien and not to waste one precious second of the five hours he had given her.

He was in fact waiting at their usual place with Sampson quite content to be inactive cropping the grass along the bank of the stream.

She ran towards him, emerging through the trees and looking, he thought, like Persephone coming to sweep away the darkness of winter.

"You are ... here!"

The words were breathless because Gracila had run so fast.

"And so are you!" he answered, his eyes on her face.

"I brought my picnic," she said, handing him the basket, "I told Mrs. Bates I had a longing to eat the peaches which have just ripened in the greenhouses."

"I have brought a special wine from the cellar," Lord Damien smiled, "and have set it in the stream to cool. I also have my rod ready to catch our luncheon as we did before."

She smiled up at him.

They were talking in a natural manner but every word seemed to have a deeper and more intimate meaning than what was actually said.

"I know what you forgot," he said.

"What?" she enquired.

"A rug for you to sit on," he answered. "It rained last night and it would be a pity to spoil that lovely gown."

"How clever of you!" she exclaimed. "I never thought of a rug."

He took one from Sampson's saddle and laid it on the short grass where they had sat before, then picked up his trout-rod.

"It would be very humiliating if today of all days I am an unsuccessful angler," he remarked.

"I think you will always be successful at anything you undertake."

"You flatter me!"

"I am not trying to do so. I am only stating what I believe."

"Once I had a few talents," he said, " 'link'd with one virtue and a thousand crimes', but now I have forgotten them."

"Then why not resurrect them?"

"What do you suggest I do?"

The question was slightly cynical and she knew that he did not expect her to answer with anything concrete that was within his capabilities.

Gracila sat down on the rug and for a moment Lord Damien thought he was blinded by the loveliness of the sun on her hair.

"I was thinking last night," she said, "of all the things you have told me about your travels. When I am alone I go over what you said and laugh at your descriptions of some of the journeys you have undertaken."

She realised he was listening and she went on:

"The story of the yaks who would not go up the mountain, the sails which tore in half during a storm in the Red Sea, the camel who ate a week's ration of food when nobody was looking!"

She laughed and said:

"Can you not see that other people who have to stay at home would enjoy reading about your adventures as I have enjoyed them?"

Lord Damien did not reply and she went on:

"Then I think I shall always remember the words in which you described the beauty of the Himalayas, the wonder of the Taj Mahal and the Emerald Buddha in Bangkok."

She clasped her hands together as she said pleadingly:

"Please write it all down! Please make a book, and perhaps some of the things you have seen would be best expressed in poetry."

"I am no Byron!"

"No, you are Damien, and as original in your way as he was in his."

She paused before she went on:

"Once I identified you in my mind with Lord Byron, but now I know you are far too individualistic and too much of a personality to be standing in the shadow of anyone else. You are you, and that is all I ... want you to be."

Lord Damien drew in his breath.

"Gracila! Gracila!" he said brokenly. "If only I had known you a long time ago! How different my life might have been!"

"I might have gurgled at you from my cradle," she replied, "or played 'Hide-and-Seek' with you in the garden, but I hardly think you would have found it particularly inspiring!"

Because he could not help himself Lord Damien laughed.

"I am being over-dramatic," he said, "and how right you are to tease me. Oh, my precious, I adore you when you make me laugh!"

"That is what I want to do," Gracila said, "so make me laugh by trying to catch a trout ... and do be careful of the trees!"

He laughed at that and did as she told him.

As she watched him she thought that no man could look more attractive or make her feel as if every beat of her heart was for him and him alone.

They cooked the trout when Lord Damien caught them, having now become more expert than they had been before.

They drank the wine that had cooled in the stream and ate the food they had both brought from the house, though it was hard for either of them to think of what they were eating.

Because she was determined not to let their unhappiness spoil their last day together, Gracila set out to make Lord Damien laugh and succeeded.

It was only when their eyes met that they often broke off what they were saying in mid-sentence and forgot everything but the nearness of each other.

At a quarter past two Lord Damien, having looked at his watch, said they should make their way to the Crows' Nest.

"Shall we take Sampson with us?" Gracila asked.

"I will lead him," Lord Damien answered, "but we can leave everything else to pick up on our way back."

Gracila drew in her breath.

When they came back she knew that it would mean their five hours were at an end and once she entered Barons' Hall she would never see him again.

Resolutely she put her hand into his and said:

"Do you realise we have never walked through the wood together? It looks so mysterious. I am sure it is peopled by fairy creatures who will watch us like intruders passing through their special domain."

"I am the intruder," Lord Damien replied. "You belong. And, my precious, you are not wholly human but part of all the mystery and wonder of nature."

"I wish that was true," Gracila answered. "When I was little I used to long to fly like the fairies, to burrow under the trees like the goblins, and lurk in shadowy places like the elves."

"I believe you do all those things," he answered.

He thought as he spoke that the tall trunks of the trees, with only occasional touches of gold sunshine percolating through the trees to rest on her head, made her look ethereal.

She was a creature from the Hidden World whose every movement was like poetry and every word she spoke like music on the breeze.

Gracila glanced at him and he said:

"I am thinking of you in a new guise and it makes me love you all the more."

He felt her fingers tighten on his and told himself that

his idea of Heaven would be to have her beside him and to know that she clung to him.

It did not take them long to follow the stream to where it turned through the trees towards the Lynmouth Estate.

Because Gracila was with him everything seemed new and different from the way it had ever appeared before.

Now there was no ghost of Phenice enticing him to follow her. It was Gracila's voice which joined with the song of the birds.

Because he was retracing the path he had trod before, he was apprehensive for a second that his memories might hurt him or confront him with the past.

Instead of which he was aware as he had never been before since he came home that Phenice was dead and she could hurt him no longer.

Gracila had filled his whole being and as he looked at her, so fresh and young, her eyes holding that special spiritual loveliness he had always sought in a woman and never found, he knew that her love had healed the wounds.

He had thought them unhealable but now he knew that though the scars might remain, they no longer had any importance.

Directly ahead of them Gracila saw the wattle fence which was the boundary.

In many places it had fallen into disrepair but it was still there and the stream running beside it was still on the Damien Estate.

Looking at the fence she could see great banks of rhododendrons just coming into bloom, and she thought that without the Crows' Nest it would be impossible to see the Queen as she hoped to do.

Lord Damien stopped and looked up and Gracila did likewise.

Now she saw high in the branches of a tall fir tree what appeared to be a platform.

"It is very high!" she exclaimed.

"Are you afraid?"

She shook her head.

"I have climbed higher trees, but I must admit not such a straight one."

"Look a little closer," Lord Damien ordered.

She did so and saw that on the tree there were little iron footholds jutting out all the way to the top.

"The lazy way of climbing," Gracila smiled.

"But much more comfortable, and certainly easier," Lord Damien answered.

He took his hands from Sampson's bridle and from the pocket of the saddle drew out a small pair of binoculars.

He swung their strap over his shoulder.

"I will go up first," he said, "in case any of the footholds have become loose. Then you shall follow me."

She smiled at him and it was with difficulty that he prevented himself from putting his arms round her.

Then he climbed quickly and without any effort up the tree, testing each foothold first with his hands, then with his feet until Gracila saw him reach the platform amongst the boughs.

"It is all right," he called. "Take it slowly and if you feel afraid I will come back and help you."

"I am not afraid," she answered almost indignantly.

She pulled up her skirt with its three stiff petticoats before she began to climb.

It had been easier, Gracila thought, before fashion decreed that women should wear very full skirts, but she was a proficient climber and the tree offered her far less difficulty than she had encountered on others in the past.

Only as she reached the actual Crows' Nest did Lord Damien reach down to take her arms and pull her up the last few feet.

It was exciting to feel his hands on her bare skin, and when finally he lifted her onto the wooden floor to be close to him for one moment Gracila could think of nothing else.

Then she looked round and gave a cry of delight.

The Crows' Nest was larger than she had expected. It had a wooden floor and the balcony extended at a radius of about three feet round the whole tree.

It was strong and substantial and there were two stools on which to sit and a small table.

"We could have had our luncheon here!" she exclaimed.

"I wanted to be with you in the sunshine," he answered.

She smiled at him, then looked out towards the gardens of Lynmouth House.

It was not surprising the second Marquess had been annoyed for the gardens lay right beneath them and Gracila could see the terrace which ran across the back of the house and the lawns which already were filled with guests.

In the distance there was a large marquee in which there were obviously refreshments and nearer to them on this side of the lawn there was a Band.

It was the Band of the Buckinghamshire Yeomanry which Gracila had heard often enough.

They were playing a waltz which made her long to dance with Lord Damien in a great Ball-room under candlelit chandeliers.

As if he read her thoughts he said:

"I feel sure you dance divinely."

"It would be ... wonderful to dance with you!" she answered.

His eyes met hers only for an instant. Then as if he forced himself to change the subject he said:

"You will be glad that I brought some binoculars, for you will be able to see the Queen's face very clearly."

He took them from his shoulder as he spoke and put them on the table.

"Before the Queen comes," Gracila said, "I will tell you who everyone is and you will be able to see how old and decrepit they have become since you last met them!"

"They would not be pleased to hear you say that."

"It is great fun to know that we can see them, but they have no idea they are being watched," Gracila replied.

She picked up the binoculars as she spoke, adjusted them to her eyes, then seated herself on one of the stools.

"Oh look!" she cried, "there is Eloise D'Arcy, the prettiest girl in the County! Do look at her!"

"I would rather look at you," Lord Damien replied.

"Perhaps you had better not look at her in case you admire her and it makes me jealous," Gracila said.

"Could I make you jealous?" he asked.

She forgot the binoculars for a moment and answered seriously:

"I think it would be difficult for either of us to be jealous of the other because what we feel is not just the idea of possession but something deeper and far more important."

"And yet you belong to me," Lord Damien said.

"That is why I should not be jealous," Gracila answered. 'I belong to you completely ... every part of me. I have nothing to offer ... anyone else."

He was very still, then he said with a raw note in his voice:

"See who else you can recognise."

Obediently Gracila put the binoculars to her eyes.

"Oh, there is Papa and my Step-mother!" she cried. "They have just emerged from the house. That must mean that the Queen has arrived."

"How do you know that?" Lord Damien asked.

"Because Papa is on the Committee of the Hospital and he and the Lord Lieutenant were to show Her Majesty around."

"Well, now you will have your heart's desire," Lord Damien said, "and see the very young but, if I have heard correctly, the very bossy little Queen of England."

"... who is very much in love with her handsome husband," Gracila finished.

"Poor man! I am sorry for him, always having to walk three paces behind his wife," Lord Damien said.

"Do you think it is a subservient position?" Gracila asked, the dimples showing on either side of her mouth.

"But of course!" Lord Damien answered. "It is unnatural. He should be the King and the Ruler."

"I agree with you. At the same time I like to think they are ideally happy."

"As we should be," Lord Damien remarked almost beneath his breath.

There was, however, no time to answer him because at that moment out from the house through the French windows came the Queen, Prince Albert, and with them the Marquess of Lynmouth.

He was an elderly man, but in his Lord Lieutenant's uniform he looked dignified and impressive.

It flashed through Gracila's mind that perhaps she had been tactless in wanting to see the Queen, disregarding what Lord Damien might feel in seeing again the man whose wife he had taken from him.

Because she felt a little embarrassed, she said quickly:

"The Queen looks lovely! She is exactly like her pictures."

"That is of course surprising," Lord Damien remarked sarcastically.

"No, she is prettier!" Gracila said. "And her complexion is wonderful. I can see it quite clearly. Do you want to look?"

"I can see all I want to see with the naked eye," Lord Damien answered. "I am sure you are thinking it is a pity you cannot hear what she is saying."

"One can guess only too easily," Gracila answered. "The Marquess is introducing the High Sheriff and his wife and now there is a whole row of County Dignitaries waiting for their glorious moment."

She moved her glasses a little to say:

"I can see my Step-mother is enjoying every moment

of it. She is wearing the gown which she bought for my wedding. I expect she had no wish to waste it."

"Think what you are missing in not being presented and meeting the Queen yourself," Lord Damien said.

Gracila turned her face to look at him.

"You know I would so much rather be here with you. I would not give up one moment of my precious hours to meet all the Kings and Queens in the world, or even the Angel Gabriel himself!"

Lord Damien laughed.

"You are very complimentary."

"I am speaking the truth."

They looked at each other. Then a sudden sound alerted Gracila's attention.

It came from below them and she thought perhaps Sampson had got his bridle entangled in a bush.

Then she saw the sound had been made by a man who was climbing through the wattles just a little to their right.

He was a tall man and for a moment Gracila thought he must be a game-keeper or a forester, even though she knew that most of those in Lord Damien's employment had been sacked.

Then she saw that though the man had common features he was dressed as a gentleman and carried in his hand a high hat.

He had managed to get through the fence, breaking further an already broken piece of the wattle and standing with a scrunching sound on those which had fallen to the ground.

"Who is he?" Lord Damien asked in a voice that only she could hear.

"I have no idea!" Gracila replied. "He is not one of your employees."

"I am certain of one thing – he has no invitation, otherwise he would have come in by the main gate."

Gracila watched the man.

Something in the way he was moving through the bushes made her think that Lord Damien was right and he was certainly an uninvited guest.

Just before he stepped out onto the open lawns they saw him put his hat on his head, pressing it down as if he was unused to wearing anything so smart.

Then he put his hand inside his breast-pocket as if to reassure himself that something was there.

He was half-turned away from them as he did so. At the same time he was also not directly facing the people he was to join.

He looked down at what his hand held, but they could not see what it was.

A sudden thought sprang into Gracila's mind and she knew as she glanced at Lord Damien that he was thinking the same thing.

"Not ... that!" she whispered. "You do not ... think he ... intends ..."

Lord Damien's expression made it quite unnecessary to say more.

He was watching the man and now they saw him begin to zig-zag through the crowds of people on the lawn, stepping round those who were talking, sliding past others, and all the time making his way relentlessly towards where the line of people were waiting to be presented to the Queen.

Beside Her Majesty was Prince Albert and behind him came an Equerry and a Lady-in-Waiting, then Gracila's father and Step-mother, and behind them again a number of neighbours, all of whom she recognised.

She had looked away from the man who had entered the lawns beneath them for only a second or two, but when she looked back at him he was now much nearer to the Queen.

"Supposing ..." Gracila gasped. "You must ... save her!"

As if he already knew it was what he must do, Lord

Damien was on his feet and, before she had finished speaking, was beginning to descend the fir tree.

He reached the ground, leapt across the stream and seemed to vault the wattle fence.

Then he was running; running through the crowds while Gracila holding her breath watched him, too tense to lift the binoculars to her eyes.

The man had pushed and sidled his way until Gracila could see now he was directly behind the line of presentations and then about ten paces from the Queen herself.

Frightened, she looked for Lord Damien and saw him running with a speed that only an athletic man could achieve.

As he pushed people out of his way, they glared at him and doubtless remonstrated, but he was gone before the words could reach their lips.

Then Gracila saw the man in the tall hat put his hand inside the breast-pocket of his coat.

The movement was quite obvious and she wanted to scream a warning even though she knew her voice would not carry so far.

Lord Damien would be too late!

The Queen was now within three paces of the man who was watching her and Gracila, with a kind of sick horror, saw him move his arm and knew what he was about to do.

She saw the sun glitter on something he held in his hand. Then even as she thought he would fire the pistol and the Queen would fall dead, Lord Damien made a desperate sprint the last few yards and flung himself on the assailant, forcing his arm upwards.

A shot rang out stopping everyone in their tracks and even the Band ceased playing.

Then the man and Lord Damien were fighting on the ground, and, galvanised from their momentary immobility, a number of Officials sprang forward.

*   *   *

If Gracila had been apprehensive, so had Lord Damien.

He had realised that the man had a good start on him and he had been delayed in climbing down the tree and having to leap the stream.

He thought that if he had had any sense he would have realised sooner that anyone who entered a private party in such a furtive way must be up to mischief.

Now, running with a speed that he had not attempted since he had won races at Eton, he zig-zagged between the guests, most of them with their faces turned towards the Queen.

He pushed his way unceremoniously through any who loomed in front of him and finally with less than a split second to spare flung himself on the man as he levelled his pistol.

It was only as the shot rang out that anyone around them had the least idea that anything untoward was occurring.

Then, as the man tried to escape, fighting violently like a cornered animal, Lord Damien flung him to the ground and held him there struggling until there were enough detectives and members of the Yeomanry who were on duty to prevent his escape.

Lord Damien stood up and pulled the lapels of his coat straight.

It was then that he found the Queen was standing directly in front of him.

While everyone else, on hearing the sound of the shot, had recoiled in horror, she, with a dignity and a bravery that was characteristic, had not moved.

Only the Prince had stepped forward as if to stand in front of her on one side while the Marquess had done the same on the other.

Now all three were looking at Lord Damien and as he bowed the Queen who was very pale but composed said, with only a slight tremor in her voice:

"I realise you have saved my life. I can only thank you."

Lord Damien bowed again. Then the Marquess said:

"May I, Ma'am, present my neighbour Lord Damien, who has been abroad for some years but has returned most opportunely and at exactly the right moment!"

The Queen smiled.

"We are glad, Lord Damien, to make your acquaintance."

Before Lord Damien could speak the Prince Consort held out his hand.

"It is difficult to put into words my heartfelt appreciation of what you have done," he said in his rather precise manner, "but I, and I know I can speak for the whole nation, am exceedingly grateful."

"It was fortunate, Your Royal Highness," Lord Damien said, finding his voice at last, "that I saw the man entering the gardens by the boundary fence."

"It was indeed fortunate," the Queen said, "and may I suggest, Lord Damien, that you should tell Prince Albert and myself more about your brave deed when we are not so occupied as we are at the moment?"

She glanced at the Prince as she added:

"I think, dearest, that Lord Damien might be persuaded to join our house-party at Windsor Castle next week, for Ascot Races."

The Prince smiled.

"The Queen and I would be delighted to see you, Lord Damien."

The Queen turned towards the line of presentations which had once more grouped themselves. As she did so the Marquess held out his hand.

"Welcome home, Virgil!" he said. "It is good to have you back!"

His voice seemed to carry so that everyone round them heard what he said, but Lord Damien knew the mere fact their hands were clasped told everyone in the County that he was reinstated.

If the Marquess had so generously forgiven him, who else would dare to cold-shoulder him?

For a moment he was too overcome to be able to reply and the Marquess joined the Queen to continue the round of duties which had been interrupted.

It was then, as if all the guests assembled on the lawn had been holding their breath, that their voices broke out in a kind of hubbub of astonishment at what had taken place.

The Band began to play again, but nothing could drown the high note in the voices arising from the shock they had experienced and a sense of excitement in having been present at a drama which might well have ended in tragedy.

One thing was in everyone's mind and that was to congratulate the hero of the hour, the man who had saved the Queen, the man who having left them so dramatically had returned in an even more dramatic fashion.

Everyone wanted to shake him by the hand, everyone wanted to add their congratulations to those of the Marquess.

As she saw the guests surging round Lord Damien, Gracila felt the tears come into her eyes and she could see no more.

She knew this was the miracle she had prayed for, this was an answer to her prayers which could only have come from God Himself.

It was so poignant that she could no longer watch what was happening on the lawns. Instead she climbed down from the Crows' Nest and taking Sampson by the bridle she led him back towards the house.

She could hardly grasp that what had happened had changed everything, Lord Damien's life, hers and their future.

When she had put Sampson into the stables she went into the house to wait, knowing that everything was now going to be quite different.

This was not the end, but the beginning.

She did not hide herself in the Elizabethan rooms but

walked along the corridors until she came to the top of the Grand Staircase.

This she descended and opening the front door which had been locked before the servants left the house, she felt now it was symbolic that it should stand open for the return of Lord Damien.

Now there was no longer any reason for him to be lonely in his own home with the door knocker not raised, the bell left unrung.

She stood at the door looking out, feeling as if the world had suddenly become radiantly golden and glorious.

And yet there was a stillness within herself and a feeling of anticipation that was so beautiful and so poignant that it was like the moment before dawn when all the world is still.

Far away at the end of the drive she saw a movement and knew as she had expected that someone was bringing Lord Damien home.

It was then that she again climbed the stairs to stand at the top of them, hidden in the shadows but being able to see him the moment he arrived.

A smart carriage drawn by two horses came to a standstill outside the house. Then she could see a footman stepping down from the box to open the door for Lord Damien.

He stood at the side of the carriage, and Gracila heard him say :

"Thank you for bringing me home, and thank you both for all you have said."

Gracila heard her Step-mother's voice reply :

"It had been a thrilling moment for us all and you will not forget, Lord Damien, that you have promised to dine with us tomorrow night ?"

"I shall be looking forward to it, Lady Sheringham," Lord Damien answered.

He bowed and added :

"Good day, My Lord."

"We will see you tomorrow, Virgil," Gracila heard her father say, "and it will be like old times to have you at Barons' Hall."

"Thank you again," Lord Damien replied.

The carriage moved off and he stood for a moment politely on the steps watching it go. Then he turned and walked in through the front door.

As he did so Gracila started to descend the stairs.

She had meant to walk down them slowly and with dignity, but suddenly she began to run and he waited, his lips smiling as she came.

As she reached the last few steps, he held out his arms.

She felt as if she flew on wings towards him, then his arms were round her and his lips came down on hers in a kiss that carried them both up into a cloudless sky.

Chapter Seven

A spray of rice caught Lord Damien on the side of the cheek and he swore beneath his breath.

Gracila laughed.

"It hurt!" he protested.

"The next time you get married you had better ask for it to be cooked," she teased, and they both laughed.

More rice poured over them interspersed with rose-petals which were far softer.

Then as they drove through the gates of the Castle there were bunches of flowers from the children and cheers from the villagers.

Gracila was holding tightly onto one of Lord Damien's hands as they waved and smiled .

When they were through the village they turned to look at each other and there was such radiance in their faces that they seemed transfigured.

Lord Damien looked so much younger, so different from when Gracila had first seen him, that it was hard to believe he was the same man.

Gone was the disillusionment, the cynicism, the bitterness. Instead he was young again and so overwhelmingly handsome that she said Byron's words in her heart:

"A Prince with fascination in his very bow ..."

It hardly seemed possible that everything she had longed for and everything she had dreamed about had come true. But now they were indeed married and, as far as the world was concerned, only five weeks after they had ostensibly met for the first time.

"What did Papa say when you told him you wished to marry me?" Gracila had asked Lord Damien.

"He was astonished," he replied, "and asked how we could possibly be sure when we had only seen each other a few times."

"And what did you say?"

"I was extremely eloquent," he replied, "on the theme of 'who ever loved that loved not at first sight?'"

She laughed, thinking of the moment when Lord Damien had come into the Salon at the Castle and had been introduced to her by her Step-mother.

She had on his insistence left Barons' Hall very early in the morning.

"I have a feeling, my darling heart," he had said the evening before when they sat together in the Library and planned their future, "that a number of people will call on me tomorrow and whatever happens they must not find you here."

"I am not afraid of what anyone can say now," Gracila answered. "At the same time I have no wish to start another scandal."

"As you undoubtedly will if it is ever known that you have stayed at Barons' Hall with me."

"It is something I never wish to forget," she said softly, "it has been the ... most wonderful ... perfect time, with a slight exception, that anyone could ... imagine."

They both knew that the 'slight exception' was when they had been forced to say good-bye to each other because Lord Damien was convinced that for her sake he could not marry her.

Gracila knew that now he was being sensible, and when they had said a passionate good-night she had agreed that she should leave soon after dawn.

"In a short while," he had said, as he held her in his arms, "there will be no more parting, no more saying good-bye ... We will be together, laughing in the sunshine all day, and at night I will hold you in my arms and teach you, my precious little star, about love."

"You have . . . taught me so . . . much already."

"What you have learnt are only the primary lessons," he answered. "There are many, many more to come."

"That is . . . what I . . . want," she whispered.

His arms tightened and he kissed her until the Library walls swung round them and there was nothing in the world but his lips and the security of his arms.

*　　*　　*

Riding her own horse, Gracila had set off at five-thirty the next morning.

Because it was wise to be discreet up to the last minute the only person to watch her go was old Millet.

Mrs. Hansell had said good-bye absent-mindedly because she could talk of nothing but Lord Damien.

Gracila realised that he had in fact become a hero overnight.

She was sure that all over the country when they read the morning newspapers women like Mrs Hansell would be blessing him in their hearts because he had saved the life of the young Queen.

She was so happy, so intent on her own thoughts, that it was only as she turned into the drive of the Castle that she realised there was something of an ordeal ahead of her.

But it did not really matter what was said because tonight she would see Lord Damien again.

At the same time she had no wish for a cloud, however slight, to overcast the sunshine which she felt surrounded her.

To her delight when she entered the Castle she found her father breakfasting alone in the Dining-room.

"Gracila!" he exclaimed. "Where have you been? I have been out of my mind worrying about you."

Gracila ran towards him, put her arms round his neck and laid her soft cheek against his.

"Forgive me, Papa," she said pleadingly. "I did not wish you to be worried. I have been safe and now I have come home and it is marvellous to see you."

She knew as he put his arms round her that he was too thankful she was back to be really angry. At the same time he demanded an explanation.

"I told you in my letter," Gracila replied, "I found I could not marry the Duke. You know that Mama would not have wished me to be unhappy."

"Why did you not come and tell me so instead of running away?" the Earl enquired.

"I thought you might say it was too late for me to change my mind, and that it would make it easier for you and everybody else if I just . . . disappeared."

Before he could speak she kissed him and said:

"Do not be angry, Papa."

"Where were you?" he asked, but she knew he was softening.

"I was with one of our old servants who looked after me very well."

"Your Nanny, of course!" he exclaimed. "Why did I not think of that? Your Step-mother was certain you would have gone to one of your cousins."

Gracila did not disabuse him by saying that as it happened her old Nanny had died the previous year. Although her Father had been told about it, he had obviously forgotten.

Her Step-mother, who had just entered the Dining-room, might have been far more difficult to mollify, but Gracila stopped the words with which she started to berate her by saying quietly:

"I had irrefutable proof that the Duke was not in love with me . . . but with . . . someone else!"

The rebuke she was about to utter died on the Countess's lips. Then as her eyes met Gracila's she understood and the colour left her face.

"Well, as you have come back we will say no more

about it," she said after a moment. "I hope that in future you will be more considerate of your father's feelings and never again upset him as you did by such an irresponsible escapade."

"I will not run away again," Gracila promised.

When the newspapers arrived at the Castle there were headlines about Lord Damien, but to her delight nothing was said as to the reason why he had left England and lived abroad for so long.

Instead the prizes he had won at school, the distinctions which had been his at Oxford, were all reported to build up his image as a dashing Cavalier who had saved the life of the young Queen.

They made him sound extremely romantic and Gracila knew that once established on a pillar of fame, it would be very hard for him to be toppled from it.

"Now he can start a new life," she told herself, "and with ... me."

It had been very hard when he came to dinner that night not to show how much she loved him and she knew that Lord Damien was as vividly conscious of her as she was of him.

Fortunately, anxious to display the new social lion she had captured, her Step-mother invited a large number of people to meet him.

It was therefore not as difficult for Gracila and Lord Damien to disguise their feelings as it would have been if they had dined *en famille.*

After he had gone the servants gave her a note that he had left for her and in it he asked her to write to him care of Millet and say when they could meet.

It had not been easy, but when they both rode early in the morning inevitably their paths crossed.

If the groom who accompanied Gracila thought it was strange, he was an elderly man who had known her all her life and could therefore be trusted not to talk.

As Lord Damien was besieged by invitations and Gracila was not only the most attractive but the most important young girl in the County, it was obvious they would meet in other people's houses.

The only thing that was needed to set the seal on his social success was his inclusion in the Royal Party for Ascot Races.

Gracila and her parents were invited to dine at Windsor Castle the night following the race for the Gold Cup.

There was dancing in the Red Ball-room, and after he had partnered the Queen, Lord Damien approached Gracila.

She was standing as was correct at her Step-mother's side and when he had bowed and she had curtsied, he led her onto the floor and put his arm round her waist.

She felt a little tremor of excitement go through her because she was close to him.

"I love you!" he whispered. "I love you and I can no longer go on with this farce. I shall speak to your father tomorrow."

"It is too ... soon," Gracila answered, but there was nothing positive in her voice.

"I want you! I want you to be mine! I want to kiss you," Lord Damien said.

The passion in his voice made her heart turn over in her breast and she knew she wanted nothing in the whole world so much as the touch of his lips on hers.

Now they were married and there was no longer reason to hide their feelings or to pretend they were mere acquaintances.

"Could anyone be more beautiful?" Lord Damien asked, lifting her hand from which Gracila had removed her glove and kissing it.

They were passing through open country but in a few moments there would be another small village where the crowds would be gathered to see them drive past.

"Did you like my wedding-gown?" Gracila asked.

"I could only look at your face and think you were not

real, but as I have thought before, a wood-nymph or Aphrodite herself."

"I have never aspired so high," Gracila smiled.

"Very well then," he said, "a star – my star – but no longer out of reach as I will show you as soon as we are alone."

He kissed her hand again and Gracila's fingers tightened on his.

"Oh, Virgil ... I am sure I am ... dreaming."

"I will prove to you that you are not, or if you are, then I am dreaming too."

Because he aroused such strange and exciting sensations in her, Gracila tried to say more lightly:

"Everyone kept asking me where we were going for our honeymoon ... what did you tell them?"

"I let them think we were going abroad," he answered. "It is what they expected."

His eyes searched her face as he asked:

"You are quite sure you are not disappointed at staying here? You know, my precious darling, that I would take you anywhere you wished to go."

"I only want to be with you," Gracila answered, "and I know there is no place you would rather spend your honeymoon than Barons' Hall."

"That is true so long as we can be alone, and I promise, my lovely one, that we will go abroad after Christmas and seek the sun in places which I long to show you."

He paused to smile before he added:

"They will also feature in the book you are determined to make me write."

"I intend to help you with it," Gracila said, "but now just at this moment all I want is to ... listen to your voice, to ... realise we can be ... together without ... fear, and the ... sands of time are not ... running out."

Lord Damien gave a sigh as if he released the last tension within himself.

"We are so clever at being secretive," he said, "that no-one will know where we are. I am also confident that Millet will stand like an angel with a flaming sword, not turning us out of Eden but keeping other people from coming in!"

They both laughed at the idea and when they found Millet waiting for them alone at Barons' Hall Gracila ran towards him and kissed him on the cheek as she had done once before.

"M'Lady!" Old Millet stammered. "This is the h . happiest day of my l . life."

"And ours," Gracila said. "And it is all thanks to you, Mitty. If you had not taken me in when I came to you with nowhere else to go, this would never have happened."

There were tears in his eyes as Millet looked first at Gracila, then at Lord Damien. Then he asked:

"Is Your Ladyship atelling me you and His Lordship met while you were staying here?"

"Yes, Mitty, but nobody must ever know it but you. We trust you."

"God's been good, very good, M'Lady," Millet said, and was too overcome to say any more.

Mrs. Hansell was also crying tears of happiness as she helped Gracila to change from her 'going-away' dress into the prettiest evening-gown in her trousseau.

"I've never seen such a beautiful bride as you made, M'Lady," she said. "You looked like a real fairy princess, or an angel stepped right out of Heaven. There wasn't a woman in the congregation without tears in her eyes!"

"I loved my wedding!" Gracila replied, "and now I shall have my honeymoon in this beautiful house which means so much to Lord Damien and to me."

"You can trust Millet and me to see that no-one knows where you're hiding, M'Lady," Mrs. Hansell said. "Just as His Lordship asked, there's only the old servants in the house who'll not intrude on you."

"Thank you," Gracila said.

"Then when you're supposed to return," Mrs. Hansell went on, "like His Lordship's instructed us, Millet and I'll engage as many servants as is necessary to make the place as fine and grand as it was in the past."

That meant, Gracila knew, that the top-floor Bedrooms would be opened, there would be six stalwart footmen in the Damien livery, and Millet would empty the safe of the Damien silver for every meal.

It was wonderful to think of it and there was so much to look forward to, but just for the moment she could think of nothing but two people – Virgil and herself.

It was an inexpressible joy to eat together in the Dining-room where before he had dined alone while she had also eaten alone upstairs.

Tonight the table was decorated with white roses and she knew that Lord Damien had chosen them because he thought she looked like that flower herself.

The candles in the huge gold candelabra sparkled on the diamond necklace which had been his wedding-present and the stars, another present, which she wore in her hair.

She had exclaimed with delight when he had given them to her, knowing that lying side by side on blue velvet they held a very special message.

She had worn them on her wedding-gown and her engagement ring was a star sapphire set with diamonds. She thought that nothing could be more beautiful.

But even so the presents were unimportant.

What mattered were the feelings that vibrated between them so that they knew without need of words that the marriage service had joined them together so spiritually that they were in reality one person.

When dinner was finished Lord Damien refused the port which Millet offered him, and hand in hand they walked from the Dining-room through the Salon and out onto the terrace.

The sky was still crimson and gold in the setting sun and the lake reflected its colour, the leaves of the trees shone with it while the shadows beneath them were growing long and purple.

"It is so lovely," Gracila exclaimed, "and it is all yours!"

"That is what I was thinking myself," Lord Damien said, but his eyes were on her face.

The smile she gave him was, he thought, the most perfect thing in the world. He linked his arm in hers and drew her down the stone steps and onto the lawn.

"Where are we going?" she asked.

"Where do you think?"

"To our ... own place?"

"Of course! Where else could we go tonight? I believed I should never see it again – perhaps never return home."

"Forget all you have suffered," Gracila pleaded. "We might have known that a Divine Power would look after us, keep us for each other and find a miraculous way for us to be happy."

"Are you happy?" he asked.

She laughed softly.

"Could you really be asking me such an absurd question when you know that I am so happy I want to sing, dance, fly into the sky, and dive into the lake!"

"That is how I feel too," he said, "and yet I am still afraid."

"Afraid?"

"That I have still not been punished enough and that I am unworthy of anything so perfect as you."

She put her cheek against his shoulder in a loving little gesture.

"You are being very humble all of a sudden," she teased. "I think I prefer you when you are awe-inspiring and haughty as I thought you were when I first saw you."

"Haughty?" he questioned. Then he laughed.

"Of course – 'his rising lip reveals the haughtier thought.' Do I still appear like that?"

"No, and I think I soon realised it was only a pretence … a facade … and I found your … secret spirit."

" 'Man is himself – the secret spirit free,' " Lord Damien murmured, but added: "I have been cheated! I am not free! I am enslaved, captured, enthralled and imprisoned for evermore."

"That is what I want you to be," Gracila said, "but what shall I do if you ever get bored? If you want to go back to your 'wine, and women, mirth and laughter'?"

"You have forgotten the next line," Lord Damien replied. " 'Sermons and soda water the day after!' "

Gracila chuckled with laughter.

"That is easy. But I doubt if you would listen to my sermons."

"Never!" he said firmly.

By now they had reached the stream. The trees shadowed it so that it was silver rather than gold and seemed mysterious as it moved towards the darkness of the wood.

They stood under the tree where they had first met and Gracila waited for Lord Damien to take her in his arms, but he said:

"This is where my whole life changed, where I looked up to find a runaway star."

"Supposing," Gracila said in a low voice, "you had ridden on and I had not been … brave enough to … stop you?"

"I should have turned back because fate had taken a hand in the lives of both of us," he said, "and, my precious one, how grateful I am that we were both so privileged."

He looked down at her, then very gently he took her in his arms.

She raised her face to his, her lips inviting his kisses, but for the moment he only looked into her eyes.

"You are so beautiful!" he said. "So pure and unspoilt! I can only say again I am unworthy."

"I love you! We love each other and I belong to you."

There was a sudden radiance in her eyes and a note in her voice that was very moving.

Lord Damien's lips sought hers, and for the moment it was a kiss of reverence and homage, a kiss in which he dedicated himself as if he was a Knight ready to serve her.

Then as he felt the softness of her mouth beneath his, as he felt a little quiver go through her, his kiss became more passionate, more demanding, a fire burnt in his eyes and swept through his body.

"I love you! My darling, my precious little star, my heart, my soul, my wife!"

Then he was kissing her until she vibrated with emotions she did not know existed and sensations which exceeded her dreams and her imagination.

He kissed her neck, her shoulders, then her lips again.

"Oh ... Virgil ... Virgil" she murmured as if his name was a talisman to which she clung.

They suddenly realised that they were almost in darkness amongst the trees and looking up at the sky they could see the stars were coming out and there was only a very faint glow left of the setting sun.

"You are 'clad in the beauty of a thousand stars'," Lord Damien quoted in a deep voice, " 'but we will go back'."

"And we will go back ... together. That is what is so very ... very ... wonderful!"

Gracila drew in her breath before she cried:

"Oh Virgil, if you only knew how I ... dreaded the thought of going ... back to the house ... alone when the five hours you had given me as a present ... ended."

"And now instead I have not given you five hours but five billion years, and even that will not be enough to tell you how much I love you or how much you mean to me."

"Do you think ... when we both die that we will ... find each other again as we have ... found each other now?"

"You can never leave me," he said, "for we are one person. Of that I am sure!"

"That is what I want to ... believe."

"I have a lifetime in which to prove it to you."

They had moved as they talked, back onto the lawn and now for a moment they stood still looking at the house standing in front of them, seeing the light in some of the windows and the starlight beginning to turn the roofs to silver.

"Our ... home!" Gracila said almost beneath her breath.

"You will make it the home I have not had for so many years," Lord Damien said, "and perhaps one day, my dearest dear, it will be a home for our children."

"They will never ... be lonely as you have ... been," Gracila promised.

"And as you have been lonely too."

"It would have been still ... lonelier if I had not read about ... you in my ... books and ... dreamt about ... you in my dreams."

"And you are not disappointed by the reality?"

She looked up at him and he saw the smile on her lips.

"How could I ever be disappointed with you? I love you so ... overwhelmingly and ... every breath I take seems to make me love you more."

"My darling! My precious one!"

Lord Damien kissed her again.

Then as they both realised they wanted to be closer still they began to walk more quickly towards the house.

The window in the Salon was open for them, but when they went into the Hall there was no-one there and with their arms entwined they walked up the curving staircase.

Tonight Gracila was sleeping in the room next to Lord Damien's in the Master Suite.

She had a feeling as they moved towards it that all the women who had slept there before her were giving her their blessing and wishing her happiness.

As Gracila had half-expected, there was no Mrs. Hansell waiting up for her and no Dawkins for Lord Damien.

He came into her room to stand looking at her in the light of the candles that were lit beside the bed.

For a moment neither of them moved. Then he asked:

"You love me?"

"So much ... so very much ... my darling Virgil!"

She moved towards him as she spoke and put her arms round his neck.

He pulled her against him, kissing her in a way that she felt was different from the kisses he had given her before.

She knew without being told that everything that was sensitive and spiritual was aroused in him, besides a fire which was very human and at the same time purified by the rapture within his soul.

He took the necklace from around her neck and the stars from her hair.

Then as he held her mouth captive she felt his fingers undoing the back of her gown.

It slipped to the floor and her petticoats followed it.

As he kissed her neck, her shoulders, then her breasts, he said:

"My star, my one precious little star, your love shall lift me into the sky from which you came. I adore you, I worship you, but I want you!"

"I ... want you ... too," Gracila tried to say.

But there were no words in which to express the love which carried them as if on a shaft of starlight into the ecstasy of their own Heaven.